Cherry Crossing

MONTANA MEADOWS: BOOK ONE

LISA M. PRYSOCK

Magnolia
BLOSSOM

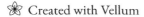 Created with Vellum

Acknowledgments

Making a book happen is a tremendous collaborative team effort. First, I'd like to give God all the glory. Thank you to my husband and family for the constant support they give me in my writing endeavors. My husband is the best plot fixer on the planet.

I'd also like to thank everyone at Magnolia Blossom Publishing for the wonderful support they provide behind the scenes. Nick, Megan, and Kaitlyn keep me smiling and laughing as we work through the publishing process. They are true professionals, full of encouragement, and super fun! A huge shout-out to the cover designer, marketing, and editing teams! Thank you for all you do. I'm honored to work with each of you.

Thank you to the amazing ARC readers who lend their support to the book launch process. I couldn't do this without you. You are simply the best!

Thank you to my writing friends, Danni, Tina, Marlene and so many more who inspire and cheer me on! You're my go to and I'm honored to know each of you. There are so many I'd like to name here, but the three I have named ... we talk almost every day. You are integral!

Thank you so much to the readers who support me on social media and with notes, letters, emails, cards, purchases, kind reviews, encouragement and all kinds of love. Writers love this stuff and where would we be without you? I love y'all!

Lisa

Theme Verse

~

"For I know the plans I have for you," declares the Lord, "plans to prosper you and not to harm you, plans to give you a hope and a future."

~

Jeremiah 29:11, NIV

Chapter One

No hour of life is wasted that is spent in the saddle.

—Winston Churchill

The spring of 1877 brought as much hope as it did a debacle of obstacles for both Jocelyn Elizabeth Hayes and the incumbent president, Rutherford B. Hayes. While he set out for Washington, D.C. with his family not knowing if he'd won the election, Jocelyn, or Josie as everyone called her—and no relation of his —wondered what lay in store for the year ahead, not only for the nation, but for the future of Cherry Crossing. The fields needed to dry out after the heavy rainfall, but the *Farmer's Almanac* prediction of drought caused her to peer outside the front windows while biting her lower lip. The previous day's events nagged at her, and Josie pulled her crocheted brown shawl closer around her elbows when she turned away from the chill at the window to pace.

At least they didn't have any more snow to contend with this year, but usually, Montana winters stayed far too long, over-staying their welcome far into May. Shivering, she hoped they'd seen the last of snowflakes and snowdrifts. The birds returning from their southern vistas to sing their songs of hope and joy to the world as they sought refuge in the apple orchard, the cherry orchard, and the trees behind the cabin told her spring had truly arrived. She took note of a few early glacier lilies, several hyacinths, and crocus blooms, too. The daffodils and tulips would shoot up a little higher and add their bursts of yellow and pink to the flower beds any week now, and she knew Ma would smile from heaven to see how pretty the garden looked.

"Josie, if you don't relax and trust God, those crease lines in your forehead will be permanent." Jacqueline's rocking chair creaked softly near the fireplace. She held an embroidery hoop steady in her hands while she worked away at what she hoped would be a fancy pillowcase like the one she'd shown Josie and their other sister, Jillian, in the latest edition of *Godey's Lady's Book*. "Why don't you join Jill and me for a little pleasant sewing or reading, perhaps? Our morning chores are done, but it's too cold and muddy to take a walk. It looks like it might rain for a week, and you're wearing out the floorboards."

"I wish I could relax as easily as you, but I can't forget, the world itself seemed to conspire against our plans for Cherry Crossing yesterday." Josie stopped pacing long enough for Jillian to cross her path to the sitting area from the corner book-cases where she'd searched for a book to read from amongst the new ones now proudly displayed on the shelves Pa had built before his passing. The new books had arrived in time for Christmas in a small crate from Uncle Edwin in Minnesota. The three of them had passed much of the long, hard winter devouring the novels, but a few remained for their reading pleasure. Jill carried her selection to sit at one of the two wooden parlor benches drawn up to the fireplace, opening a copy of *The Mill on the Floss.*

Josie resumed pacing. "It has me questioning everything we've worked so hard for."

"Did you know George Eliot is a woman?" Jill, the youngest of the three sisters, held up the copy of an American edition of the book in her hands, closing it again momentarily to admire the spine and cover bearing the title and author's name. Then she glanced over her shoulder at Josie with a sweet smile, one finely arched, dark brow rising to hear Josie's response.

"Hmm? Yes. Yes, I did." Josie's barely audible reply came as a testament to her distraction. Normally, this clever line of discussion and thought process of her darling youngest sister would have enticed Josie at once. Every bone in her body wanted to be a writer. Nothing invigorated her more than a healthy discussion about books or writers. She often spent her treasured spare time scribbling her ramblings onto paper, but not today. No, today, she couldn't shake the mixture of melancholy and anger at her predicament.

Ignoring Jill's question, Josie continued. "I have wrestled about the matter all night long, tossing and turning, doing my very best to find forgiveness in my soul. The best I can do is to forever regard Miles Brooks and his horse farm with mild distaste and complete distrust. Anyone who would outright sell a promised horse to someone else on the day before an agreed upon appointment is most wretchedly inexcusable indeed. He knew I was on my way there on the appointed day and agreed upon time, and he knew I had worked for months at the mission to save for the purchase. Although he had reluctantly agreed to give me extra time to raise the sum he required for the purchase of Blue, he had agreed to wait until yesterday, and then he broke his word."

Jackie looked up from her sewing. "Indeed. A man who breaks his word cannot be trusted. Pa always said so. A man's word is all he has."

"And what of the man who bought your horse?" Jillian inquired.

"It would have been my horse, but whoever bought him out from under me, he is no friend to proceed with the purchase of the desire of a lady's heart, thereby disrupting a prior arrangement. Brooks and I had no written contract, but we had a verbal agreement. Even here in the wilds of Montana Territory, a gentleman's agreement is generally respectable and binding. Miles Brooks wouldn't have done what he did if I were a man." Josie's fists clenched as she considered the matter.

"Blue was such a nice name, too," Jill lamented and bent her head down to read. She opened the book in her hands, turning to the first page. "He would have made a fine first stallion for our future champion herds at Cherry Crossing."

Jackie bit her lip, looking up from the pillowcase she spread across her lap. "What are you going to do, Josie?"

"I'm going to pay Mr. High and Mighty Swindler a visit and convince him to sell Blue to me," she replied, pausing from pacing where her brown skirts skimmed the clean, pine floorboards, "whoever he is. I can't imagine why he would have bought my horse, unless Brooks didn't tell him, of course, in which case he may not think himself so smart to have swindled me out of my horse."

"How will you find him?" Jackie asked.

"I don't know, but I'll find him. Honey River Canyon is a small town, and I know exactly what Blue looks like. Miles Brooks may not have been willing to tell me who he sold him to, but the buyer can't hide for long on a horse like our Blue. The future of our farm depends upon finding him." Josie sighed and plopped onto one of the plank benches, drained from all that had happened.

"There's new sheet music for a waltz in the latest *Godey's* edition if you'd like to play something to take your mind off all this," Jackie said softly. "I put it on the piano."

"Thank you, Jackie. You're a dear." Josie smiled weakly and turned toward the instrument. At least Ma's upright piano offered her some creature comforts. Besides the church and the mayor's mansion, they were among the only farmers she knew of who owned a piano in all of Honey River Canyon. She'd simply have to push her troubled thoughts aside for now and head to town when the weather didn't look quite so dismal and dreary. Surely someone had seen a man riding about on the horse meant for her.

Chapter Two

Truth carries with it confrontation. Truth demands confrontation; loving confrontation, but confrontation nevertheless.

—Francis Schaeffer, an American evangelical theologian, philosopher, author, and Presbyterian pastor

It rained on and off for the next two days. When Jocelyn needed to escape the confines of the cabin, she went outside to chop firewood under the fenced awning extending on one side of the barn. Winter had depleted much of their extra supply, and when the Martin brothers didn't come to help chop wood for them, she had to work hard to keep up with what they needed for the cookstove and the fireplaces on the first and second floors. Her upper body lacked the strength to swing an axe for

long periods of time, so she approached the task in brief incre-
ments. As the eldest daughter, the chore mainly fell to her since
the blizzard had stolen the lives of their parents after her seven-
teenth Christmas. She'd never trust a January thaw ever again,
but she had resigned herself to raising her sisters and carving out
a good living on the farm for them—with their help and coop-
eration.

The arrangement required hard work and dedication. Both
good and bad days had followed, but the circuit judge had
chosen leniency and indulged their desire to remain together
since Pa had left a will, leaving the three of them the farm. He
and Ma had proven up on the claim, filed for the deed, and
collected it. The girls hadn't seen their paternal Aunt Louisa or
maternal Uncle Edwin in years. It had made no sense to the
judge to pack three girls off to Minnesota when in a few short
months following the tragedy, Josie would turn eighteen and
could look after them herself.

Now, at twenty-three, with Jacqueline at twenty, and Jillian,
nineteen, the three of them had reached the legal age of adult-
hood. Sometimes her sisters grumbled about the hard work, but
for the most part, they'd accepted their lot, especially since they
didn't want to return to Minnesota to live as dependents on
family they barely knew. After all, they were established in
Honey River Canyon. They had friends, neighbors, and many
who checked in on them, helping at planting and harvest times.
It made the hard work bearable, and the girls made many of the
decisions jointly, like the one they'd made to acquire horses for
Cherry Crossing.

When the rain finally stopped, Josie donned her Sunday
best, a rose-colored gown with the lovely bustle she'd copied

from a free pattern included in a summer edition of *Godey's Lady's Book*. She slipped into her cape, hooked the button at the neckline with the braided loop, and then pinned the matching straw hat in place over her wavy brown hair.

"I'll return in time for supper. I'm going to see what I can find out about who has my horse since the rain has stopped," Josie told her sisters as she drew on her white gloves, pulling them snugly to her wrists.

"Be careful, Josie. I don't think this reprieve will last for long. It's still overcast and gray out there." Jackie nodded in the direction of the window facing the dormant kitchen garden where rolling clouds loomed, each one appearing angry in the big sky looking down on Cherry Crossing.

She shrugged and muttered, "I'll hurry." Then she left them in the kitchen paring potatoes and carrots for a stew, hoping they wouldn't forget to make biscuits, or maybe a delicious pie or cobbler for dessert. Too early for fresh huckleberries or black-berries, they still had some apples and jars of canned berries in the cellar. She could hardly wait to get to planting so they could enjoy some fresh fruits and vegetables.

Josie hummed a little tune as she hitched up the wagon behind Violet and Vera, careful to step around the mud and softer ground. She used a lap blanket to protect her dress from splatters, and snapping the reins when she'd positioned herself on the seat, she quickly steered the team down the drive toward the dirt lane leading to town.

On the way to Honey River Canyon, she went over her plan. First, she'd scour the streets and avenues in town, looking for any sign of Blue, pausing to speak to a few townsfolk for any news if she saw anyone. If this approach didn't produce the desired results, she'd begin searching the countryside. She'd begin on the southwest side of town, working her way in a large circle toward the north where Cherry Crossing lay, sprawling out from the base of Silver Mountain.

The town spilled out from the base of eight splendid and majestic mountains wrapping around the northwest corner. Honey River, named for the way it gleamed like golden honey at sunrise and sunset, wound its way through the eight mountains, twining around them, this way and that. Josie didn't care much for fishing, but Pa had always said some of the best trout in North America came from Honey River. He'd brought plenty enough of it home for Ma to fry up for their supper over the years. Although small, the community consisted of an adequate and growing number of shops, businesses, farms, and even a little industry with a thriving dairy farm and two mills springing up alongside Apple River, one for flour and the other, lumber.

In addition to looking for her horse, she needed to settle an account with the butcher and purchase some tea and sugar at the general store. Situated only a few blocks from the town square, the stop would give her an opportunity to thoroughly search Church Avenue. However, when she arrived at the butcher, she could hardly believe her good fortune to spot the beautiful black stallion. Unmistakably sleek and lean, the mustang appeared to be in excellent health. Not only did Blue appear well, but the gentleman dismounting from the shiny leather saddle certainly appeared in fine health. His golden-blond hair and blue eyes met her gaze as he nodded in her direction when she pulled the wagon into a parking space beside them. Indignant because he had her horse in his possession, she could only offer a curt nod in response. The stranger strode toward the hitching post to tether the beauty.

The man—a stranger in town—finished tethering the reins and hurried inside, likely to purchase a delicious pastry from the owner. They offered huckleberry cobbler and cakes nearly year-round, owing to their diligence in canning the delectable berries in great quantities during the summer months. Pies, scones, streusels, tarts, and sweet breads graced their menu, along with soups, tea, spring water, lemonade, and coffee. Today, the aroma of freshly baked apple pie wafted into the street when the stranger opened the door to duck inside.

Josie wasted no time in jumping down from the wagon. What if he just happened to be passing through? What if she never saw Blue again? This could be her only chance. She quickly tied her team to the hitching post and followed, ready to give him a piece of her mind. The bell on the door jingled when the door closed behind her, and a quick glance around at the empty tables and chairs gave her some degree of relief. At least they were alone, except for Mrs. Delia Williams, the bakery owner emerging from the kitchen to stand behind the counter at hearing the bell ding not once, but twice. She looked positively delighted to accept their orders, but Josie paid her no mind.

"Good afternoon. May I help you?" Delia asked the stranger as he studied the variety of confections on display in the bakery case.

"I'll try a slice of the apple pie and a cup of black coffee," the man said.

Josie marched right up to the stranger, putting herself partially between him and the counter, ignoring the scent of cinnamon and cloves mingling in the air. "No, you won't," she heard herself say without thinking. She placed her hands on both hips and tapped one foot on the floor.

The stranger turned to look at her with some surprise. "Y-yes, I most certainly will," he sputtered, looking from her back to Delia. "And I'll have one of those huckleberry scones, too." The man withdrew some coins from his pocket and reached around Josie, placing them on the counter firmly, proving he could pay for his purchase.

Delia's mouth hung open at hearing Josie's intervention of the man placing a simple order for a slice of apple pie. Josie raised a gloved hand to stop Delia from interrupting and held it up toward the counter. Keeping her eyes on the stranger, she tilted her chin. "Oh, no, you won't. You can keep the coins and wrap his order up for later, Delia. I have business with this... this..." Josie looked him up and down, trying to decide if she should use the word swindler as she had at home. Noticing his clean white shirt, suspenders, clean trousers, and the brown tweed suit coat he'd slung over one shoulder, she reluctantly added, "gentleman."

Anger flashed in the man's eyes briefly. His eyes softened and half a grin settled into an amused look on his face. Josie didn't see what seemed so funny, but she soon caught onto the idea he considered her a nuisance when he waved her aside and shook his head. "I don't have any business with you, and with manners like yours, I'm not sure you qualify as a lady."

Josie felt heat rise into her cheeks as they burned a shade of red. Ignoring his declaration, she continued. "You most certainly do have business with me. You're going to sell me back my horse, the one you swindled from Miles Brooks which was promised to me."

The stranger glanced over his shoulder outside the front windows of the shop toward Blue. The horse flicked his tail as if he had something to say about the matter. The stranger's chest puffed out as he stood up taller. "I most certainly will not, and he is not *your* horse. And I did not swindle anyone, as you put it."

"Yes, he is my horse, and Brooks shouldn't have broken his word. We had an arrangement, and I was and still am prepared to keep my end of the bargain, although he has not kept his word." Josie crossed her arms over her chest and tilted her chin up.

"I don't have anything to do with whatever happened or did not happen between you and Brooks. It's your problem, not mine. Now, if you'll excuse me, I'd like to eat my pie in peace." The man stepped closer to the counter, effectively side-stepping away from her.

Delia quickly slid the man a saucer with a slice of apple pie on it. "I'll get your coffee and scone, sir. I'll bring it out to your table if you'd like to have a seat." The bakery owner shot Jocelyn a pleading look, silently begging her not to continue the argument with her customer.

Josie's fists clenched as she turned on the man, marching out of the store, allowing the door to slam behind her. *Way to go, Josie.* It hadn't gone well. She should have tried a different approach, but as usual, her impetuous nature had gotten the better of her. Encountering him had happened so fast, and she hadn't taken the time to think any of it through.

Chapter Three

This is all the inheritance I give to my dear family. The religion of Christ will give them one which will make them rich indeed.

—Patrick Henry, American patriot

Jacob Hunter stared after the brunette beauty as she stomped off to her wagon where he could see a team of nice-looking chestnut mares waited to remove her from his vicinity. The bakery owner brought him the promised coffee and huckleberry scone. He hadn't tried huckleberries before, but their bright purple color looked appealing, except for the fact he could hardly enjoy them after such an unexpected confrontation. Thinking his grandfather wouldn't approve, he hadn't come to Honey River Canyon to rile any of the inhabitants.

"Who is she?" Jake asked before the matron of the shop could step away from the table he'd chosen beside one of the front windows where he could keep an eye on his stallion. He didn't trust the brash girl.

"There goeth Jocelyn Hayes," Delia Williams replied, "otherwise known as Josie in these parts. I don't think I've ever seen her so angry and determined before. She and her other two sisters were orphaned when her parents were caught unawares in one of those Montana blizzards popping up out of nowhere. She's the eldest of the three girls. Practically worked her fingers to the bone raising her sisters. 'Tis why she's skin and bones."

He nodded, and Delia scuttled away to wait on someone else entering the bakery, but Jake stared after Josie as the wagon pulled away. He didn't know why the horse meant so much to her, but from the sounds of it, Brooks had done her wrong. Still, it wasn't any of his fault. The horse belonged to him now, and he couldn't help it if Brooks had broken his word to her. He hadn't known anything about their arrangement. Shrugging, he turned back to the piece of pie in front of him and reached for the fork, trying to push the incident from his mind.

Mrs. Emmerson placed the sack of sugar and the tin of tea on the counter. "Anything else for you today?"

Josie didn't hear her question as she looked over her shoulder, staring outside the general store windows in case the stranger followed her. Mrs. Emmerson had said something she'd missed, but she had no idea what. Turning back to the establishment's owner's wife, she fished out the sum required and mumbled, "Thank you," dropping the coins in her hand.

The coins clanked as Katy Emmerson added them to the till and handed her the change. "You look like you've just seen a ghost, Josie. What's ailin' you today?"

Josie tucked the change in her drawstring purse and pulled the strings tight to close it. "Oh, it's this fella I saw at the bakery. Miles Brooks sold him the horse he'd agreed to sell me. Broke his word to me, he did. I don't think I'll ever trust him again, Mrs. Emmerson."

"How awful," Katy replied with a cluck of her tongue. She leaned forward. "Did you say you saw a fella at the bakery with the horse you wanted?"

Josie nodded. "I did. He's about, oh, maybe twenty-five or twenty-seven, blond hair, blue eyes, kind of handsome..." Her voice trailed away, and she bit her lip. Perhaps she shouldn't have remarked upon his looks, but it was true. The stranger had been tall, strong, and muscular with a finely shaped jaw, a strong nose, good cheekbones, and the kind of tan one achieves from working hard on a farm. The good Lord knew she struggled dearly to keep her bonnet on to preserve her creamy skin. At least she and Katy were alone in the mercantile where no one could overhear her words and repeat them. "I've never seen him before, but Brooks sold him my horse, all right. A beautiful black stallion."

"I know you must've had your heart set on him," Mrs. Emmerson said, empathizing with her. "I meant the horse, not the man."

Josie ignored the remark about the man, but it did cause

one of her brows to rise. "I surely did. The Lord knoweth." She sighed, lamenting the entire situation.

"This fella on the black stallion does kind of sound like the mayor's grandson," Mrs. Emmerson informed her. "He arrived on the stage a few days ago. I think the first thing he did after settling in was to come in here to ask about where to buy a good horse. Of course, everyone here told him to go see Miles Brooks and his horse farm."

Josie's mouth dropped open as she clasped a gloved hand over her mouth. Rolling her eyes, she sighed. "Oh, dear... the mayor's mansion has been empty for three whole months. I forgot someone might come to claim his estate eventually. I do seem to remember the colonel's wife mentioned they had a grandson he'd never met. Estelle was a true lady, and I miss her so. I might not have said anything to him had I known..." Her voice trailed away.

"Don't tell me you confronted him, Jocelyn Hayes." Katy Emmerson peered at her.

"I may have," Josie admitted. She dismissed her actions with a wave of her gloved hand. "Oh, dear. What's done is done." She reached for the tin and the sack. "I'll try to make it right later. Right now, I'm plumb mad at the world."

Katy Emmerson sighed. "Can't say as I blame you. If Brooks promised to sell me a horse and then sold it to someone else, I'd be hotter than a magpie in August. Everyone knows you've been working hard at the mission all winter. I imagine it took months to save up for a fine horse."

"It did. I scrubbed floors, cleaned, washed the laundry, helped with the cooking, and even taught French lessons to the orphans." Josie paused from staring at the pickles in a glass jar on the counter making her mouth water. She turned and looked up at her friend behind the till. "Maybe you've seen the mayor's grandson on the horse after he purchased it."

"I have noticed him on a fine black stallion. Kind of hard to miss a beautiful horse like him with a rather nice-looking gentleman riding straight through town. Jake Hunter—he told us to call him Jake—has been out riding every day since he bought the stallion. Getting to know Honey River Canyon a bit, I suppose. I didn't know it was the horse promised to you."

Josie could only nod, saddened by the reality of the situation. "I'll see you later, Mrs. Emmerson. Please give my regards to Clark and the children. I guess we'll simply have to figure out some other way to find a black stallion."

She gathered her purchases into her arms and carried them to the wagon, tucking them under the front seat before climbing into it, being careful to tuck her dress in under the blanket again. Driving home, she knew she had to let it all go somehow, as heartbroken as she found herself. Finding a pure black stallion to match her black mare had turned into a formidable task. This Jacob Hunter didn't sound like he'd sell Blue to her as she had hoped. He stubbornly wanted to keep the horse, even though she knew his dearly departed grandfather, a colonel and the former mayor, had plenty of other fine horses in his stables behind the mansion.

She'd chosen the name Blue because of the blue sheen glimmering on the black stallion's coat, but none of it mattered now unless she could strike a deal with the mayor's grandson and pay stud fees. She didn't have any intention of doing so, which meant she'd need to change her requirements for a stallion or keep looking for another. Settling for a less than perfect beast or waiting until another black stallion came along did not appeal to her in the least, but what choice did she have. *Lord, are you there? I could use a little help down here.*

"You mustn't let this fellow upset you so, Josie. I can hardly believe you found Blue." Jill slid a cup of hot tea in Josie's direction. "Here, drink some of this. You'll catch your death in this chill. It's such a rainy, cold spring this year. I'll put another log in the cookstove." She rose from the plank table in the kitchen and reached into the wood box for another log from those Josie had worked so hard to split. Sometimes it boggled Josie's mind to think of how much wood she'd chopped since the horse she'd had her heart set on had sold to some other bidder. Chad and Charlie usually kept their supply of firewood high, stopping by frequently to chop wood for them. Even they'd be surprised at how much she'd chopped.

"Ma and Pa would be proud of your efforts to turn Cherry Crossing into the finest horse farm in all of Montana Territory. We'll find another horse to match our champion mare." Jackie clutched a cup of tea from her seat at the table, adjacent to Josie. "I can't believe you confronted the mayor's grandson! I know it seems hard to believe, but we will eventually find another black stallion somewhere."

"I hope so, but it's the eventually part I don't like. We need our own stallion, and the sooner the better. We can't afford to pay stud fees." Josie clamped her jaw firmly closed to keep her teeth from chattering. She'd missed a downpouring of rain by minutes, and the chill outside had taken a toll on her. Thunder clapped in the distance. Only time would tell if her errand had profitable results. Maybe this Jake Hunter would prove to have a heart and change his mind about selling her the horse after he had some time to think on it, the one glimmer of hope she kept tucked inside her heart.

"Having a fine horse farm was something Pa had talked about so many times. He wanted Cherry Crossing to be the best one possible, but it was all he could do to prove up the claim and build this cabin for us to have a nice roof overhead. There's got to be a way to make Pa's dream happen. We need quarter horses of all kinds, truth be told, and eventually, maybe some thoroughbreds."

"I guess it's not only Pa's dream anymore," Jill said. "It's become our dream, too."

Jackie nodded, and Josie couldn't help but smile at Jill's words.

"Do tell us what happened," her middle sister said, leaning forward. "We want to hear every word. Does the mayor's grandson despise us all now? Are we to become outcasts in Honey River Canyon?"

Josie rolled her eyes. "Oh, p'shaw, Jacqueline Hayes. 'Tis not so bad. It was merely a business discussion, but I daresay we don't like each other. He's too arrogant and stubborn in my opinion."

"And we all know our big sister isn't proud or stubborn," Jackie replied, smirking.

The kitchen grew quiet until Josie burst into laughter with them. When she stopped laughing, she added, "I can be positively wretched, and I'm afraid I was exactly that today."

"It's not like you didn't have reason enough," Jacqueline commented, trying to console her.

Josie finished relaying her account of the encounter with the mayor's grandson. Jackie's brows furrowed after hearing the story, and then her brown eyes lit up. "Perhaps we can bake something for him as a sort of peace offering... at some point." Jill remained pensive, considering the situation in silence, staring at her teacup. "Maybe some huckleberry scones or apple pie."

Josie shrugged and sipped more of her tea. Setting her cup down, she clasped both of her hands around it for warmth, glad to finally be home from her excursion. Having told her sisters about her folly, she at least felt some relief to have shared the matter. "I don't know. Clearly, he likes apple pie and maybe huckleberry scones too, but I think we should let him stew for a few weeks in the hope he may reconsider the matter."

"I feel as though I am not doing enough to help make our horse farm a reality." Jillian sighed, toying with her teacup in its fine China saucer, one of Ma's cherished possessions she'd left behind for the girls to enjoy.

Josie looked at her youngest sister and shook her head. "I won't have you feeling this way, Jill. We agreed you would pursue your teaching certificate. Your studies come first. Once you have obtained a teaching position, you'll be able to buy a new horse for our stables every three months, and possibly more often. Your plans to become a teacher are vital to our success. Eventually, you'll surpass us with what you'll be able to do for Cherry Crossing."

"Jocelyn is right." Jackie nodded. "I'm afraid 'tis I who am letting us down, but when I marry someone wealthy and generous, I shall be able to do more than purchase one horse a year with the little I am able to earn by taking in extra sewing."

"If any of us can marry well, it shall certainly be you, Miss Jacqueline. Ma gave you a name fit for a princess, and you have the natural beauty to go with it. I have great faith in your plans, but do leave room to consider your heart. Not that I speak from experience since I can't say I have ever truly been in love, but I've read more books about love than both of you put together. Sometimes ladies fall in love with someone who isn't anything like what they may have imagined or hoped for."

"I am certain I shan't like anyone well enough to marry if they are not stunningly wealthy." Jackie toyed with the lace trim at the sleeve on her blue calico. "I only want to have pretty dresses, do some good in this world, take care of my family, and never trouble myself about hardship and toil ever again. You shall both be welcome to live in my beautiful estate as your summer house or second home whenever you like."

At this assurance, her sisters smiled and laughed. Jackie always had her head in a daydream. Josie shook her head, seeing it as her responsibility to keep her sister mindful of reality. When the giggling subsided, she added a light admonishment. "Do try to keep your feet firmly on the ground, dear sister. I worry you will be greatly disappointed in life if you don't find this elusive, rich fellow to marry someday. Leave room for other possibilities. We live in the wilds of Montana Territory, surrounded by countryfolk and farmers."

Jackie rose, crossing the kitchen to the cookstove to fill three bowls with some of the beef stew. It had simmered for hours, filling the kitchen with the delicious aroma on the rainy spring evening. They'd dine in the small kitchen by the warmth of the cook stove rather than in the front room at the larger table. "It is so very hard, but I do try not to desire a rich husband too terribly much. Really, I do. You have no idea how hard it is for someone like me who only ever dreams about fine hats, parasols, pretty dresses, and having shoes to match each gown. Yet here I am, in this humble station in life."

"I have no doubt you will be the first of us to marry astonishingly well. While this humble station sums everything up for now, yet in His infinite wisdom, the good Lord knew what He was doing when He chose you for us." Josie scooted forward in her seat when her sister handed her a steaming bowl filled with gravy, carrots, potatoes, onion, and tender pieces of beef. The chattering in her teeth had stopped, and thankfully she had decided she would not ponder the matter of the stallion any longer. Tomorrow she would only lament having to look Mrs. Velvet in the eye and tell the rescued mare she had failed to find her a suitable mate. For now, she would enjoy having dinner with her sisters and think about spending the evening writing at her desk in the solace of her bedroom where she could hide her disappointment.

At least they still had their chestnut mares, Violet and Vera, who looked noticeably beautiful when pulling the wagon. They also had Chicory, a brown and white quarter horse who could plow a straight furrow better than most. Josie had great hopes Chicory and Violet's foal they'd named Gallant would make the beginnings of a fine herd. Gallant, born last summer, possessed a healthy chestnut coat like his mother, with fine white markings on the nose and legs, like his father. She hoped they would find a mare to mate with Gallant, but she found the reality of keeping up with space to house them and producing enough hay and oats to feed them, daunting.

No wonder horse farms didn't spring up like dandelions. Still, she wouldn't allow their dreams to fade away. They'd need to work toward building a stable. She could picture Ma and Pa smiling at their progress. Josie had a strong feeling her parents could look down from the windows of heaven every now and then.

Chapter Four

Beware how you trifle with your marvelous inheritance, this great land of ordered liberty, for if we stumble and fall, freedom and civilization everywhere will go down in ruin.

—Henry Cabot Lodge, American politician, born 1850

Jake Hunter returned to the mayor's mansion after his visit to the bakery, still thinking about Jocelyn Hayes. The stubborn, insistent beauty kept returning to his mind as he wandered about the great house, trying to get to know his grandfather through the possessions he'd left behind. He couldn't help but wonder what his grandfather might have done in this situation, but he also prayed for the Lord to give him wisdom. As he stared at his grandfather's portrait above the fireplace in the library, a Scripture kept turning over in his mind about caring for the widow and the orphan. It nagged at him until he realized he'd raked his hair several times as he agonized over the purchase, his grandfather's steel blue eyes peering straight ahead, a stoic and unreadable expression on his face.

The housekeeper, Mrs. Maddie Penworth, knew more about his grandfather than he did it seemed. He wanted nothing more than to sit down with her and Arthur and ask them to tell him everything they could think of concerning Colonel Harrison Lee Bradshaw. They had countless stories about him in their memory banks, but it wouldn't seem proper, he supposed. He had sat down a time or two with Maddie and Arthur in the kitchen over a cup of black coffee, and they'd shared a few anecdotes and things with him. If only he'd asked his ma to tell him more about her mother and father before she'd passed. He remembered her telling him several stories about his grandparents, Harrison and Estelle, but they seemed to run together in his mind at present.

He wandered down the hall into the music room and sat down at the grand piano, playing a portion of a lively concerto by Bach. He wondered if Estelle or his grandfather had played from the very sheet music he now read as his hands glided across the ivory keys of the beautiful instrument. Crisp, clear notes rang out, and he enjoyed the sound emanating from the expensive heart-shaped piano. It fascinated him to find his grandfather had succeeded in finding a way to have it transported this far west. He guessed few settlers had a piano, let alone one like this.

He wondered if his grandmother, Estelle, had played the instrument, and figured perhaps his grandfather had purchased it for her. If so, he guessed he had loved her deeply. Maybe someday soon he would find a love like they'd obviously shared. He could see fine touches all around the mansion testifying to his love for Estelle, including several portraits of his bride at various ages, plenty of jewelry and trinkets on her dressing table, and fine furnishings throughout the home. A staff of servants to help them care for every need and desire lurked in every corner, causing Jake to wonder when he might ever find privacy again if he continued to keep them on staff.

He stopped playing abruptly and closed the lid over the keys. How would he live up to his grandfather's legacy? Already, Maddie and Arthur had asked if he'd run for mayor. Besides this, he'd poured over his grandfather's ledgers several times, trying to understand how he could manage such an estate and a sum left to him in the local bank coffers. Having grown up a simple farm boy, it overwhelmed him, even though he'd obtained his preaching certificate from a fine school back in Philadelphia. If folks knew he'd lost his first position as an assistant clergyman because he'd boxed Esquire Phineas Lawrence's ears, punched him in the jaw, and broken his nose, they might toss him out of town on his own ears.

As much as he regretted the fact the church board had sacked him and sent him packing on account of his temper, he didn't regret starting a fight with Phineas after Clara Whitehall had deserted him, breaking off their engagement to pursue marriage to an attorney. She obviously hadn't loved him as he'd loved her. It came down to money, he supposed, the root of all evil. If only Clara could see him now, surrounded by this luxury in the Wild West. She'd wish she would have stayed at his side since now he'd inherited his grandfather's estate. He blamed Phineas for stealing her from him. Yet after all that had transpired, he couldn't fault Clara. She only wanted the best future possible for herself, and an assistant clergyman with a meager salary, living on his Pa's farm, hardly compared to the earnings of an established attorney like Phineas.

Jake wandered through the grand ball room, looking at the black and white floor tiles— imported from Italy, Maddie had said. He wouldn't have come to Honey River Canyon he supposed, if not for these events. In fact, he'd stared at the letter from his grandfather's estate for weeks, reluctant to leave his widowed father behind in Philadelphia to manage their Pennsylvania farm. In the end, leaving his sullied and ruined reputation behind for a fresh start in the wilds of Montana Territory had won out over the other arguments in his mind. He'd boarded a train to carry him as far west as possible, and at the end of the line near the Mississippi, he'd taken an Overland Coach northwest to reach his destination. Thankfully, his father seemed to have understood, but Jake could still see his father standing there at the train station, turning his hat in his hands when they'd waved good-bye to each other.

Now he only felt lost in the mansion. What would he do with these large rooms and all these fine furnishings without someone to share it with and a family? Would the town vote for him if he ran for mayor, or would they want to give some other local fellow a chance? In the end, he only wanted to preach the gospel, but did the town even need another preacher? He had yet to ask but hoped to find out. Then again, maybe the good Lord had other plans in mind for him since he hadn't proven he could control his temper. Maybe pursuing another position as a clergyman would only lead to someone digging up his past. Maybe he'd messed up what he'd felt called to do, and now he'd have to choose an alternate path in life. Time would tell, he figured.

And why had his grandfather not accepted his mother's marriage to his father? Hadn't he loved his daughter and wanted her to be happy with the person she'd chosen to marry? Had all this wealth ruined his good judgement? Hadn't his mother said her father had wanted her to marry some cattle ranching king, but she'd run away and eloped with a simple farmer instead? He supposed they would have visited his grandparents if it hadn't been for two things, distance and disagreement. In any case, he had this chance before him now. If only he could figure out the best way to use the opportunity for God's glory, and maybe get to know his grandfather a little through his legacy.

The woman who'd confronted him in the bakery came to his mind again as he wandered through the double doors of the ball room into the drawing room and stood back to admire the ornate carvings and moldings around the fireplace as a parlor maid scurried away, surprised at his entrance. He vaguely recalled her name as Polly from the day he'd arrived when Maddie and Arthur Penworth had lined up the servants in the hall for introductions. Ignoring the parlor maid who'd dropped her feather duster as she abandoned her post, his mind returned to the encounter with the brash, outspoken woman at the bakery. Jocelyn Hayes—or rather Josie—certainly had pluck, his mother would have said. He didn't want to marry someone like her, nor someone afraid of her own shadow like Polly. No, he wanted a peaceful union, but there had to be someone on earth who would complete his life, if only the good Lord would make her known to him. How on earth had he accomplished a dispute and managed to upset another female like he had Clara after only arriving under a week ago?

He'd only wanted his own horse, and not one from his grandfather's stables. Maybe his decision to buy a horse had been somewhat frivolous, considering he owned eight of them now. What would he even do with eight horses? Enjoy them, he supposed. Still, the purchase of a horse had seemed perfectly understandable to him. Every man needed his own noble steed, and he'd had to leave behind a good one in Pennsylvania. Other than perhaps a new suit and hat or two, he couldn't see the need to make other purchases anytime soon.

He shrugged off the guilt this Josie foisted upon his conscience and headed for the kitchen. Surely, he'd find the housekeeper there, although the house could easily have him running in circles to find anyone because of its size. He'd ask Mrs. Penworth or any servant he could find to serve him dinner in the library by the fireplace, and then he'd read a book to take his mind off this blasted woman's fury about his horse. His grandfather's collection of books could make a small town's library green with envy. He may as well make good use of it.

Chapter Five

In the spring at the end of the day, you should smell like dirt.

—Margaret Atwood, Canadian poet, novelist,
literary critic, essayist, inventor, and teacher

Three weeks later when the weather had warmed considerably, Josie and her sisters walked toward Main Street to dine at Anne's Kitchen. For now, matters about the horse farm mattered little. Spring planting had settled upon them. They'd decided to splurge and have dinner in town to celebrate the fact they'd finished the task. The winter wheat had been harvested, and the spring wheat fields sown. In addition, two fields each of corn and seed potatoes had been planted, and the entire kitchen garden. They would soon have peas, lettuce, snap beans, peppers, squash, cucumbers, tomatoes, sweet corn, cabbage, sweet potatoes, watermelons, and much more to feast upon. The hay looked almost high enough, and Josie guessed the first cut could happen in May. She'd learned to use Pa's scythe and a wooden hay rake as well as almost anyone could.

She and her sisters had worked hard, but a visit from Chad and Charlie, the eldest Martin brothers and sons of the most successful cattle farmer in the area, had helped them finish the planting considerably sooner than expected. As they had in previous years, the neighborly brothers had shown up early in the morning and worked until sundown for several days, helping them plow up the fields and broadcast seed in swaths for the wheat and corn plantings. The potatoes required more painstaking precision, but the crop yield would be good, and they'd not starve even if they sold seventy percent of the hearty spuds.

At the end of each day of plowing and planting, Josie and her sisters went to bed sore and tired. She'd fallen asleep as soon as she sank into her pillow at night. Her hands felt rough and calloused though she'd worn work gloves. Although Chad and Charlie had maneuvered the plow for them in their fields, using the garden hoe and the new secondhand tiller they'd recently acquired had taken a toll on her hands. Her back and knees ached from bending, crouching, and kneeling to drop seeds in the ground. She had to wrap her hands from the blisters, but they would heal soon enough. As she covered some of the seeds with the rich, fertile soil, she felt a kind of satisfaction when they'd finished their work as she surveyed the tidy rows of their long kitchen garden. Standing at one of the upstairs windows in her bedroom, she could admire their fields and pray for the Lord's blessing over the coming fall harvest.

For now, she'd successfully evaded Chad's request to escort her to the spring dance, but Jackie had accepted Charlie's invitation. This meant all their middle sister talked about on the way through town had to do with what she'd wear to the event. Because they lived on the neighboring farm to their east, they'd always been close to the Martin family. The fact the Martins owned one of the largest farms in the area and were considered among the two or three wealthiest families in Honey River Canyon caused her sister to be enamored with Charlie.

Josie, however, worried incessantly about the fact they'd be delighted to absorb the land Cherry Crossing had to offer. It might make the Martin clan owners of the largest farm in all of Madison County. Pa had pointed this out to her long ago, and since he'd remained cautious in his regard for the interest the Martin boys had for his daughters, Josie remained staunchly reserved about any of them placing their heart's affections on a Martin. In fact, she occasionally reminded her sisters of Pa's position on the subject, but Jackie usually brushed the concern aside. "I'm only a middle sister. It wouldn't matter if I married Charlie. I'm only one-third of Cherry Crossing, same as for you, Josie," Jackie would say. Maybe her sister had a point, but still, something nagged at her whenever the Martin boys came calling.

"Do say we can stop at the milliner on the way home, Josie." Jacqueline fussed with the bow on her bonnet as they progressed toward the restaurant. They'd purposely parked the wagon outside the library to enjoy the walk since the weather had warmed. They only needed light shawls for the evening.

"They'll be closed by the time we're finished with supper," Jillian pointed out.

"Yes, but I want to peer inside the windows and see if they have acquired anything I'd like to attempt to fashion for myself. The right bonnet or a new hat makes all the difference in the world for a true lady to look stylish and modern," Jackie explained.

"We can stop for a few moments if you don't dawdle for too long," Josie agreed, nodding when Chad Martin waved to her from the hardware store as they turned the corner onto Main.

Chad had pursued Josie for years, and the fact he'd never given up on her despite the numerous times she'd pushed him away remained a testament to his persistence and determination. Her sisters swore it was on account of the fact most townsfolk considered Josie among the prettiest girls in all of Madison County. Still, a few concerns about Chad's character and his motives caused her to continue to have reservations about him. Sure, he'd bestowed her first kiss and escorted her to her first dance, but Josie always wondered if she'd find true love elsewhere. Montana Territory's big sky told her the world existed in a much larger space than the vast span of acres the Martin clan claimed. She usually relented and accepted Chad's invitations to dances and other town celebrations, but sometimes she said no to keep him at bay and her own feelings in check.

The three sisters, dressed in their going-to-town finery, made an eye-catching sensation together. Today, Josie thought they looked their best for the outing. She had an extra spring in her step as they walked. They needed to look as nice as possible since she'd confronted the mayor's grandson on her last visit to town. What if she ran into him again? She should at least make every effort to appear polished and smart so he wouldn't think her rude and uncivilized simply because she'd confronted him, and they lived in the untamed Wild West.

Partly because of the previous incident, and partly because of the beautiful weather and their celebratory mood, she wore her favorite coral dress paired with a stunning hat. The hat, trimmed in peach and coral flowers, had a little cream netting to cover her eyes. She felt beautiful whenever she wore it. She'd copied the gown two summers ago from one they'd seen in the town's seamstress shop window. It featured a peach and cream calico overskirt drawn into a fine bustle over the coral skirt. The bodice, with its perfect fit to complement her figure, featured peach satin-covered buttons and two vertical rows each of calico and lace trim. Though not brand new, the ensemble looked exceptionally nice, and she seldom wore it except on special occasions.

A little while after they'd turned the corner onto Main Street and walked nearly a block toward the restaurant, a covered wagon pulled by a team of chestnut horses came barreling down the street toward them at a dangerous and reckless high speed. The man steering the wagon hollered, "Yee-hawww!" Then he aimed a shotgun up in the air and fired, yelling again, "Yeee-haw!"

Josie and her sisters—along with anyone else walking on Main Street—froze in their tracks, mouths agape. Seconds later, the man fired off another shot. This time, everyone outside, along with the Hayes sisters, dove for the deck of the boardwalk in front of the shops or dodged indoors. Some hid behind barrels, water troughs, wagons, or anything they could find for cover. They heard screaming and cries from the others on the street, and their own gasps and cries.

The wagon rumbled past them leaving a trail of dust whirling in the street, but Josie found herself pummeled to the ground as she tried to cover her sisters and push them out of harm's way. It felt as if she'd been run over by a steam locomotive, the wind knocked out of her as she gasped for air. Looking over her shoulder before she could yet breathe, her eyes widened in surprise to find Jake Hunter on top of her as she lay on a pile of skirts belonging to her sisters. All four of them were in a heap on the boardwalk, huddled beneath the windows of Miss Adelaide's Jam Company across from Anne's Kitchen.

Chapter Six

Bullfighting is the only art in which the artist is in danger of death and in which the degree of brilliance in the performance is left to the fighter's honor.

—Ernest Hemingway, Nobel Prize-winning author

Torn between the fact the handsome Jake Hunter had knocked her to the ground like a bull racing toward a Spanish matador, and the fact he'd managed to cushion her from the blow by placing one arm around her slim shoulders, Josie sputtered between gulps for air as he stood and then offered a hand to pull her from the heap.

"What on earth?" Jacqueline exclaimed as Charlie Martin caught up to them, eager to assist her. "Who was that fellow?"

"I have no idea," Charlie answered as he helped Jackie

stand.

"Mister Hunter! Y-you... scoundrel! You knocked the wind out of me!" Josie heard herself exclaim when she'd finally recovered, vaguely aware of Sheriff Casey Drummond in hot pursuit of the wagon, his horse thundering down Main Street past them. Heaving, she reached up to return her hat to its rightful position atop her hair.

"Aren't you going to call me a *swindling* scoundrel?" Jake Hunter asked with a twinkle in his blue eyes as another amused grin appeared on his face.

Josie blushed, remembering she'd called him a swindler at the bakery, and now she'd added to the blunder by calling him a scoundrel. Flustered by the situation and her own actions, she disregarded his response as she continued to brush herself off and set things to right again. Jake tried to help brush some bits of hay and dust off her skirt, but she shoo'd his hand away with further indignation, stepping back to put some distance between them. Still gasping for air, she tried her best to regain her composure.

When she finished brushing herself off and could breathe easier, she stood up straighter, realizing he stared at her with a funny look in his twinkling eyes. Was he chuckling softly at her? What could he possibly find so amusing? She didn't see anything funny at all.

"What?" she spat, feeling her carefully coiled hair to find whatever held his attention as he continued to stare at her.

"It's just..." he reached out gingerly and brushed something away from her hair, "a little straw in your pretty hair."

Josie clamped her mouth shut, realizing her sisters and the Martin boys were watching the interaction between the two of them closely. Chad approached, only a few feet from them, and she could feel his intense scrutiny. Most folks in town considered them an item, but only because Chad Martin paid her so much attention. She hadn't given him any indication she belonged to him, and for some reason, it seemed important to her to establish her independence around the stranger who infuriated her so much.

"We haven't had this much excitement in Honey River Canyon since I can't remember when." Jillian accepted Charlie's hand as he turned and helped her to her feet.

"There goes the sheriff!" Chad huffed, reaching Josie's other side as he caught up to his younger brother. "Are you all right, Josie? You're not hurt, are you?"

"Thank you, Chad. I'm fine now, I think." Josie looked from Chad to Jake, wondering how the two most handsome men she'd ever seen in all of Madison County stood at her elbows, fussing over her. Despite the fact one of them behaved like a troublesome stranger, and the other she held in lukewarm regard most of the time, their attentions did comfort her in an odd sort of way, mainly since Pa wasn't around to look after her and her sisters anymore.

"Are you all right, Jill?" Jackie asked, smoothing her lavender overskirt. "You were under all of us."

Jill winced and rubbed her right elbow. "Just a little sore is all. I'll be fine. It's Josie I'm worried about. She had the wind knocked out of her and is barely recovered."

"Yes, I did," Josie mumbled with a nod, staring at Jake in disbelief as she tried to straighten her hat one more time. She didn't know whether to thank him for trying to shield her from a stray bullet or slap him for knocking her over.

"My apologies, everyone." Jake looked down the street in the direction of the wagon as the sheriff caught up to it. They all craned their necks to peer with him, wondering if the man in the wagon would surrender his weapon. Jake shook his head and continued. "I'm afraid I didn't know where he would aim next, and it wasn't until he had nearly passed us when I realized the driver is one of my friends from back home in Pennsylvania making a grand entrance. He's always wanted to go west, and since he's now here, I think he must be of a mind to have some harmless fun and got carried away."

"Harmless fun!" Josie put her hands on her hips, hardly believing her ears. Did Jacob Hunter think shooting at the townsfolk and reckless driving qualified as harmless fun? She immediately regretted the words escaping her mouth and clamped her lips shut, biting her lower lip. Did she detect Jake turning a little red? She really must learn to keep her mouth shut. She'd embarrassed the stranger, and yet she hardly knew him except for the fact he was the former mayor's grandson.

"Yes, well…" Jake removed his hat and scratched behind his ear. "He sent a telegram a few days ago saying he'd visit, but I had no idea he'd be this happy to see the Wild West. He's probably read one too many stories in the papers. He's normally more reserved than this. I'll have a stern talk with him."

"Looks like the sheriff has things well in hand," Chad said, clapping Jake on the back. "He's pulled the wagon to a stop, your friend put his shotgun away, and they're talking, but your friend will need to do some mighty fast talking to get himself out of this with only a warning. Sheriff Drummond don't take kindly to anyone disturbing the peace."

"I guess I should go and see if I can spare a few words to save

Hugh Stanton from having to see the west from inside a jail cell." Jake turned back to the ladies. "If you'll accept my apologies for knocking you and your sisters to the ground to save you from any stray bullets, Miss Hayes." Jake looked pointedly at Josie, leaving her speechless before he turned to the others, "and as I said before, my apologies to all of you for Hugh's behavior." He nodded and slid the hat back on his golden-blond hair. "If you'll excuse me, ladies and gentlemen, it appears I am needed elsewhere." Then he turned and sauntered off at a leisurely pace toward his friend and the sheriff.

"Well, I never," Josie muttered under her breath as she stared after Jake. She turned back to her sisters a few seconds later, shaking her head. "Let's have dinner, shall we? Would you care to join us, gentlemen? We were headed to Anne's Kitchen before the excitement." At least Chad and Charlie behaved like true gentlemen, she decided. She may as well be friendly and invite them to join them for dinner, but her thoughts couldn't help but ponder on the fact the handsome grandson of the former mayor who now resided in the beautiful mansion facing the town square had attempted an act of chivalry to assist them. Perhaps he would have done so for some other ladies, but presently, no other ladies strolled on this block. His actions left her in a state of wonder.

"Dinner at Anne's Kitchen sounds nice. Whaddya say, Charlie?" Chad asked.

Charlie nodded, placing a huge smile on Jackie's face as she intertwined her elbow in his. He winked at his older brother. "Sure, I'm famished, and Anne makes the best pot roast this side of the Mississippi."

Chapter Seven

A friend is someone that knows you as you are, understands where you have been, accepts what you have become, and still, gently allows you to grow.

—William Shakespeare

"I'm going to give your friend a warning, but this will be his only warning." Sheriff Drummond turned to Hugh. "Do I make myself understood? If it weren't for the fact you're the colonel's grandson's friend, you'd be spending the night in a jail cell for disturbing the peace and wanton endangerment to the good people of Honey River Canyon."

"Yes sir. It won't happen again," Hugh promised, an apologetic look on his face.

"All righty, then. See that you don't test me." The sheriff

tugged on the reins in his hands and turned his horse in the opposite direction, riding away to see to other matters, leaving them in peace. Jake heaved a sigh of relief for his friend.

"Good Lord, Hugh! You tryin' to get me in a heap o' trouble?" Jake chuckled and climbed up into the wagon. "See the big house at the end of the square, 'tis my grandfather's mansion. We can park at the stable behind it, and I'll have Maddie serve us up something fine to eat for dinner, but you must promise to be on your best behavior."

"Sure thing, Jake. Sorry, I guess I was just excited to finally be here. I didn't realize you'd have a sheriff this far west. I bought the wagon and the team of horses after the train dropped me in the middle of nowhere since I didn't like the idea of riding in a stagecoach, packed in tight like peas in a pod for days on end. It's been a real long drive ever since. I don't know what I was thinking when I arrived, except I had finally reached the western frontier." Hugh laughed as he snapped the reins on the horses, gently this time. He elbowed Jake good-naturedly. "It sure was fun though. Something to write home about." Then he whistled as he took in the view of the mansion. "Wow-wee! Look at that fine house. You must be richer than my Pa."

"It is good to see you. I admit I was surprised when I received your telegram. Speaking of the judge, how did you talk him into letting you head west? He'll be missing your help on the farm, and your ma will, too." Jake knew Judge Stanton and his wife, Sarah, would have died of embarrassment if they'd witnessed their son come through Honey River Canyon in such a brazen manner.

"He was none too happy about it, to be honest," Hugh

admitted, "but since I've been restless of late, and because you and I attended the Philadelphia School of Theology together, and since we have been neighbors all of our lives, Pa relented. He said maybe it would do me some good to sow my wild oats before I settle down into marriage with Gwendolyn."

"I'm awfully proud of your engagement to Miss Smith. Don't do anything to mess that up, ya hear? Miss Gwen is a real fine catch for you, and she loves you more than Miss Clara loved me, in spite of all the efforts your ma made to invite her to Philadelphia on my behalf. Who knew she'd run off after Phineas Lawrence?" He recalled the hospitality Mrs. Stanton had shown by providing an invitation to Miss Clara Whitehall to stay at their country house so his former fiancée could meet his father. The arrangement had also allowed Jake to spend more time with his betrothed since she lived farther away. Jake had taken her for romantic walks on the grounds at Judge Stanton's farm, picnics, and horseback riding. He wouldn't have been able to do any of those things so easily after his mother's passing without a female hostess to make it proper. Hugh's mother and father had made the visit possible and socially acceptable. He'd only had to make a short drive over to his friend's estate each day from his own farm. His mother would have liked Clara, at least until her fickle nature had surfaced.

"Yeah, I sure didn't see that coming. I'm sorry things turned out the way they did. I guess Phineas turned her head at the dance. Better to find out now than after marrying, as I said before." Hugh's words showed empathy and then he changed the subject. "I'm glad to finally be here. It's been an interesting journey so far. I set up a campfire every night, hearing the wolves howl when I went to bed, and trying to keep away from the black bears. Followed along with a wagon train most of the way."

Jake nodded, lost in thought as he recalled the moment when Clara had met Phineas at the dance Mrs. Stanton had held in honor of their engagement. Sometimes he wished he could forget entirely. Though the memories had begun to fade, they still surfaced, and it pained his heart to recall the way Clara had looked at Phineas. Why had it taken him so long to accept it?

Hugh looked around at the mountains in the distance, taking in some of the countryside beyond the edge of town. "You'll find true love out here in the beautiful wild of Montana Territory. Just look at those mountains and all this fine land surrounding Honey River Canyon. Country girls are the best. I think they are raised with better values. Gwendolyn seems thankful for any advancements in life I can offer her. Clara was a city girl with high ambitions. Don't waste your time lamenting her." Hugh steered the wagon past the post office and hardware store, straight ahead toward the drive leading behind the mansion.

Jake nodded, thinking he certainly had found a belligerent beauty in the lovely Miss Jocelyn Hayes. She had looked prettier than any of the single ladies he'd seen in town so far, and especially today. If only he could tame her tongue, the brunette vixen might prove Hugh's statement about country girls correct.

Did the other fellow who joined the fray outside Miss Adelaide's Jam Company lay claim to the beautiful Miss Josie? He couldn't help but wonder. For now, he pushed the thought aside as the wagon pulled up to the stable and two of the employees his grandfather had kept on staff appeared, ready to care for his guest's team and wagon. He hadn't expected to run into Miss Hayes so soon, not while his conscience wrestled about the purchase of his horse. He'd only hoped to take a leisurely stroll through town to clear his mind and maybe visit some of the shops, but now he would turn his attention to entertaining his old friend and neighbor from college and childhood days. After all, he might not have any other visitors from back east for many years due to the rigorous journey.

Hugh, accustomed to having hired help from growing up as the son of an important figure in the community, grinned as he jumped down from the driver's seat. Coming around to the other side, he clapped Jake on the back after reaching inside the wagon to retrieve his portmanteau. "If Clara could see you now, she sure would be sorry. The ladies will fall at your feet, my friend."

"That hasn't exactly been my experience so far." Jake chuckled, thinking about the dressing down he'd received from Miss Hayes, twice. They headed inside, stepping around the kitchen garden by staying on the stone path leading to the mansion.

"Give it time. You haven't been here long enough, but once word gets out..." A twinkle appeared in Hugh's eyes as Jake led them further along the path to the rear entrance. "I'm not a wagering man, but my guess is you'll be engaged before Christmas."

A vision of Josie wearing a wedding veil danced before his eyes, captivating him for a few seconds as they passed a few clumps of Iris and daffodils. They climbed a set of steps leading to a side door and stepped inside to a foyer. "And when is your wedding to Gwendolyn? Have you two finally set a date?"

"We are to wed in late June, and Gwen insisted on my fitting for the morning suit before my departure." His friend rolled his eyes as they placed their hats on a marble-topped side table. "She's in hog heaven planning every last detail."

"I bet your eyes glaze over every time you hear the word wedding." Jake enjoyed his turn to laugh and heckle his friend.

Hugh nodded. "I told her to tell me when to arrive and where to stand, but it only got me into trouble, and I still have no idea why. I thought the ladies wanted us gents to stay out of the way when they're planning a wedding, but they wanted my opinion on the flowers, the cake, a wedding photo, the reception, the guest list. On and on... and none of it makes any difference to me as long as we are together and happy for the rest of our days."

"That's the hope, my friend, that is the hope." Jake led Hugh inside the kitchen through a door on their left so he could have a word with Mrs. Maddie Penworth about his guest's arrival and their dinner. He could smell something wonderful simmering on the cookstove. Everything halted as employees stood from their chairs and stopped in their tracks to stand at attention upon his arrival.

"Clara doesn't know what she's missing," Hugh mumbled, a smirk on his face as he elbowed Jake.

"May I help you, Master Hunter?" Mrs. Penworth stood in the center of the kitchen near the main worktable with a large basket of flowers and vases spread out before her on it. Customarily, she used clippings she cut from the garden to create floral arrangements for various rooms in the household, and he could see she had a knack for the task.

Jake smiled, glad to find her there. "Ah, yes. If you would be so kind as to show my guest and friend to one of our best guest rooms and prepare a hot bath. Then we'd like to dine in about thirty minutes in the formal dining room. He has had a long journey from Pennsylvania, and I think he'll be anxious for a homecooked meal immediately after he has had a chance to refresh."

"Of course, I'd be happy to do so. I believe you approved the meal of roast beef, boiled potatoes, creamed peas, spring greens, buttermilk biscuits, and apple pie earlier this week for tonight's menu," she reminded him when he raised a curious brow toward the cookstove.

A smile spread across Jake and Hugh's faces. Jake nodded. "Yes, very good. Thank you, Mrs. Penworth." As the house-keeper led his friend away, he made a mental note to pay a little more attention to the weekly menu the next time she brought him one requiring his signature; yet another reason why he should find a wife.

Chapter Eight

With upright heart he shepherded them and guided them with
his skillful hand.

Psalm 78:72

Jacqueline, picking up her pace when she saw Josie and her younger sister in the cherry orchard, cut across a meadow to reach them sooner. Josie took great pride in the flathead cherry orchard Pa had imported from Canada. He'd planted the trees and watched over them until they grew and began to produce, hence the name of the farmstead, Cherry Crossing. Likely, her older sister wanted to check their progress and inspect the delicate blooms and leaves for any potential insect damage.

"Josie, you'll never guess," Jackie began, pausing to catch

her breath when she arrived. She handed Jillian the history books she'd borrowed from the small library in town.

"What, what is it?" Josie let go of a low branch bearing some lovely white blossoms and turned toward her.

"It's Chad Martin. He's campaigning for mayor!" Jackie announced.

"Chad?" Josie's mouth dropped open. "Campaigning for mayor?"

"But what about Jacob Hunter? Won't everyone vote for him? I mean he is Colonel Bradshaw's grandson and all." Jill looked confused about the news. Her brows furrowed as she considered the matter.

Josie nodded. "That's kind of what I thought, too."

"Thus far, nobody knows if Mr. Hunter will run for mayor like his grandfather," Jackie explained as she pushed her bonnet off so it hung down her back by the long ties.

"How did you find out about this?" Josie asked, putting her hands on her hips, a curious look appearing on her face.

"He was standing in the middle of the town square this afternoon giving a speech. He said he knew the people of Honey River Canyon better than most because he was born and raised here. He promised to make the town a better place." Jackie brushed some hair from her eyes, still breathing heavy from racing across the meadow and the long walk to and from town.

"Did he now? And how exactly does he propose to do that?" Josie asked. "Did he mention a specific plan?"

"I'm not really sure. He talked about how he knew what farmers needed since he's the son of a local cattle farmer, and he said he'd work with the sheriff to keep our town and community safe. I only heard the last few minutes of his speech. It ended shortly after I arrived, but I thought you'd want to know." Jackie smiled weakly. Josie didn't appear too pleased to hear much about Chad's latest ambitions.

Josie nodded. "Yes, thank you for telling us. I'm not sure what I think about this news. I'm going to give Mrs. Velvet a good brushing and take her for a short ride. Then we can eat supper. I boiled some turnips, so we can have mashed turnips, peas, cornbread, and molasses cookies for dessert."

"I'm not sure what I think about this news either but thank you for picking up these history books for me in town. I'll begin studying them right after dinner. I'll go in and set the table while you're riding, Josie." Jill turned toward the cabin and Jackie followed.

Jackie decided it best not to mention the handsome gold prospector's brother, Abel Keller, who'd kissed the back of her hand, praising her for possessing what he'd called true natural beauty. New in town, he and the prospector had seemed nice enough, but Josie seldom trusted newcomers until she became better acquainted. For now, she decided she'd keep this information to herself, but she could hardly wait to encounter Abel Keller again. The man fairly took her breath away, and not from walking or running. He and his brother, a Mr. Cadence Keller, also looked quite well off. Additionally, his brother's wife, Florence, had invited her to stop by the hotel one afternoon for tea when she happened to visit town again.

"Of all the nerve of that Chad Martin, running for mayor!" Maddie Penworth poured some steeped tea from the teapot into her cup and plopped down into a chair in the kitchen by the large stone fireplace. "I can't imagine anyone voting for him when the colonel's grandson had just arrived." She'd stepped out onto the front porch to hear Chad's speech with the rest of the household staff. It had taken every bit of her manners not to boo and hiss at the candidate, and she had hushed the few who'd attempted to from among those employed by Master Hunter so as not to allow one of them to disgrace Colonel Bradshaw or his grandson.

"Now Maddie, you know Master Hunter is still getting to know the townsfolk. Maybe he doesn't feel ready to run for mayor," Arthur pointed out. He slid his cup toward his wife.

She peered into his empty cup. "I'm sorry, dearest. I'm so upset about hearing the Martin boy's speech, I can hardly think straight. I forgot to pour your tea." She filled his cup and placed it in his saucer. They'd taken this same tea break nearly every afternoon for the past two decades, and she couldn't remember a single time when she'd forgotten to pour Arthur his tea.

"Chad Martin isn't a boy anymore. Isn't he about twenty-five now?" her husband asked.

Sally Danvers, the cook, nodded. "Yes, I think you're about right, Mr. Penworth. He's about the same age as my Clifton. He and Chad went to school together. Of course, it was long before the colonel built and established the new schoolhouse." She sipped some of her tea and passed a plate of scones around the table. "They're huckleberry scones today."

"I'll have one." The parlor maid, Miss Jane Edwards, selected a scone from the plate and passed it to Marjorie

Smythe, the scullery maid. Marjorie did the same and passed the plate along to the others seated at the table.

"Once the town realizes how kindhearted Master Jake is, they'll surely vote for him," Miss Susan Parker said. "When Mr. Hunter arrived from Philadelphia, he authorized for every one of his grandfather's employees to remain on the payroll, including those at the trading post. None of us have lost our jobs as we thought we might. I'm ever so thankful."

Arthur nodded and selected a huckleberry scone. "How right you are Miss Parker. How right you are."

"How are we going to get him to run for mayor? If we don't, Chad Martin will drive the town into the ground. I honestly don't think he knows what is required to be a good community leader. He's a nice fellow, but there must be a reason why Josie Hayes hasn't married him yet. He's been after her for years." Mrs. Maddie Penworth eyed the scones on the plate and selected one with a sigh.

"Aye, Mrs. Penworth. I, for one, happen to agree with you. We've got to find a way to convince Master Hunter to campaign for mayor, and then we must help him win the election." Brent Tolliver, a household servant, reached for the teapot and added more tea to his cup.

"Thank you, Brent." Mrs. Penworth nodded in his direction.

Hugh Stanton emerged from near the cookstove, having slipped into the kitchen unnoticed, hoping to find something to eat. "I hope you don't mind if I help myself to another one of those delicious huckleberry scones. We don't have these berries in Pennsylvania."

"Oh, my goodness, you gave me a fright, sir," Mrs.

Penworth said as she rose from her seat at the table with the others. She recovered her composure as someone held the plate of scones up toward Mr. Stanton.

"Ah, thank you. Please do sit down everyone. I didn't mean to disturb you on your break. These are the most delicious scones I've ever tasted in my life." Hugh grinned and selected one from the plate with a wide grin as the employees slowly sank into their seats. He turned to go, but then turned back around. "You know, I couldn't help but overhear your conversation, and I too, agree with you. In fact, since my arrival, I've been trying to convince Jake to run for mayor. I see it as his duty to carry on the legacy of his grandfather, Colonel Bradshaw, the former mayor. From everything I've managed to learn about the colonel, he was quite a hero in his time. Who better than the grandson of the town's founder to carry on his legacy?"

The others at the table smiled and nodded, and Hugh continued. "I'll continue to see what I can do to encourage him to campaign for mayor before I must return to my fiancée."

"Thank you, Mr. Stanton, thank you very much," Mrs. Penworth said, her eyes lighting up with hope. When Hugh had disappeared around the corner, she paused and looked around at the others. "Maybe we can think of something more to do if we try very hard."

Chapter Nine

The greatest happiness of life is the conviction that we are loved; loved for ourselves, or rather, loved in spite of ourselves.

—Victor Hugo, French poet, novelist, playwright

Josie propped her elbows on the four-board fence to the corral behind the barn and stared at Mrs. Velvet as she pranced about and then settled for a moment to graze. "I'm not sure where I'm going to find your perfect mate," she told the horse, "any more than I'm sure of where I'm going to find the perfect mate for myself. I'm counting on the Good Lord to help us, Mrs. Velvet."

Mrs. Velvet looked up at her for a second and returned to grazing. Josie continued. "I had found the perfect stallion. I'd named him Blue, and then it all fell apart. I'm so sorry, Mrs.

Velvet, but I assure you, I have not given up. I'll find someone for you, and one day, someone will find me, as well. Someone handsome, strong, intelligent, kind, compassionate, caring, gentle, and Godfearing. He must be Godfearing, or Ma and Pa wouldn't approve."

This time, the black mare she'd rescued crossed the corral to nuzzle her nose in Josie's hand. She couldn't help but giggle. "I'm glad you haven't given up hope. I shan't, either."

A few seconds passed as she enjoyed the horse's nuzzles, patting her lovely mane and scratching behind her ears. "You know, I've decided I won't accept Chad's invitation to escort me to the spring dance. Instead, I shall go alone this year."

"Then maybe you'd consider accepting my invitation to escort you to the dance, Miss Hayes."

She recognized that voice. Josie swung around from the fence, coming face to face with Jake Hunter, wondering how long he'd stood there watching her, and when he'd arrived. How much of her conversation with Mrs. Velvet had he heard? She hadn't heard a conveyance come up the drive. "Jake! I mean, uh, Mister Hunter! Are you in the habit of frightening ladies by sneaking upon them?"

Jake sighed. He raked a hand through his hair as he held his hat with his other hand. "I'm sorry. I didn't mean to startle you. Your sister said you were out here." He glanced at the black mare behind her inside the corral as if he wanted to ask her something about the horse.

She glanced toward the log cabin, her eyes coming to rest on Blue. Something about seeing her horse again bristled her. She stiffened. No wonder she hadn't heard him drive up the lane. He'd ridden the stallion, and from inside the barn she hadn't heard him while mucking stalls. Maybe since now he'd seen the mare, he would understand why she wanted Blue. A girl could hope, she supposed.

"As you can see, I'm very busy, Mr. Hunter." Josie marched around him, away from the corral, returning to the barn, picking up a stray rake and shovel as she went.

He followed, leaning on the top rail of a stall door once inside, watching her move about efficiently. He cleared his throat. "You have a beautiful farm here at Cherry Crossing."

His voice, low and soft, surprised her. She looked up at him after putting the tools in their proper place, thinking if he'd arrived tomorrow when she had decided to work at the mission, she'd have missed his visit.

"I saw the sign with the farm's name at the beginning of the drive," he added.

How dare he look so handsome! "Thank you," she said, stepping over to apply some saddle soap and neat's-foot oil to the saddles. She began working up a lather on the first one by using some of the saddle soap, a cloth, and some fresh water from the pail she'd brought into the barn earlier. "Surely you didn't ride out here all this way to tell me Cherry Crossing is a beautiful farm."

Jake crossed the barn to her side and took the cloth from her hands, setting it aside. "No, I didn't. I rode out here to ask you to permit me to accompany you to the dance, Miss Hayes." He pulled her close into his arms, and Josie, stunned, didn't try to stop him. The attraction between them seemed undeniable and magnetic. Where she had refused to acknowledge it before, this time, as he held her close, she could not. He tilted her chin toward him and kissed her gently. Then he stopped, looking at her eyes, her hair, and her lips, tracing a finger along her face. "I'll pick you up at seven, if you'll allow me to be your escort."

She pushed him away and looked down at the saddle. "Only if you don't bring Blue. I can't bear to see him again when you and I both know he should be in my care."

"Blue?" He glanced toward the cabin. "Oh, you mean Tornado. I've named him Tornado, but all right, I won't bring him. Do you have any favorite spring flowers I can bring?"

"Spring flowers?" she repeated, dazed from his kiss, thinking none of this should be happening after what had transpired regarding the horse she needed—the horse she had wanted so much for Cherry Crossing to reach its destiny. Picking up the cloth again, she felt forced to set her thoughts aside due to the attraction between them, surprised to hear herself answer him. "I like buttercups, sweet pea, larkspur, yellow bells, geraniums, shooting stars, and hyacinths, but any flowers are fine." She didn't look up at him, keeping her attention on the saddle as she cleaned it.

Her peripheral vision caught him nod in her direction, and then he slid his hat back on over his golden hair, taking her response about the flowers as a yes. "I'll see you then, Miss Hayes." And then he strode from the barn before she could change her mind. She paused from her work and touched her lips, remembering his gentle, strong, yet sweet touch and the moment he had caressed her face. Her cheeks warmed to a shade of crimson to think of his magnificent kiss. How could she deny him?

"Do tell us what Colonel Bradshaw's grandson wanted," Jacqueline cajoled when Josie joined them inside the cabin to wash up for dinner.

"Yes, we are all curiosity," Jillian said as she set three plates on the table.

Josie sighed as she scrubbed her hands with soap and water at the basin. "He asked me to the spring dance, and I accepted."

Her sisters squealed and swarmed her at the basin. "How wonderful! What will you wear?" Jackie asked as Josie rinsed her hands and reached for a linen cloth to dry them.

Josie stepped past them and crossed the kitchen to find a cup in the hutch to pour a cup of tea. "I have no idea. I'll find something."

"I'm so happy for you!" Jillian beamed.

"Someone has asked me to the dance, too." Jackie carried a vase of wild violets to the table and fussed with arranging the blooms.

"Who?" Jill stepped over to the cookstove to check on the chicken and dumplings she'd made. She seldom made anything else when her turn to cook came around.

"His name is Abel Keller," Jackie informed them.

"I've not heard of him." Josie poured herself some of the tea steeping in the kettle on the cookstove, careful to stay out of Jill's way.

Jackie chattered on about Abel as she plucked the silverware from a drawer at the hutch and placed a proper setting at each plate. "He's new in town. He and his older brother, Cadence, are gold prospectors. Cadence Keller is married to a nice lady named Florence. We're about the same age. I met them when Chad gave his first campaign speech in town a few days ago, and she invited me to tea at the hotel. They're staying there for now. They think there may be gold in the mountains around here."

"Many people think gold might be found in these mountains," Jill remarked. "Maybe I should give up my dream of becoming a teacher and do some gold prospecting."

"Don't give up your dream, Jill. Wealth doesn't always lead to happiness, and I'm sure you're meant to be a teacher." Josie sat down at the table. Turning to Jillian as she joined her, she asked, "Did you have tea with Florence at the hotel when you went into town today?"

Jackie nodded. "I did. What a fancy set of rooms they have. It's like a suite with two bedrooms, a parlor to receive their guests, and real carpet on the floors. Mahogany furnishings and everything. Anyhow, before I left, Abel escorted us downstairs to the hotel foyer and asked me to the dance."

"Just be careful. They are still strangers to us." Josie placed a linen napkin in her lap the way Ma had taught them. She knew nothing she could say would lead her sister to steer clear of the gold prospectors at this point, and she supposed no harm could come from a friendship, at least not yet. Besides, at age twenty, Jackie could make her own decisions. "Let's pray. I'm famished."

"Well, how did it go? Did she say yes?" Hugh asked as he leaned forward in a chair in the library, eager to hear the rest of the story.

Jake smiled as he held a cup of tea in his hands. "She did."

"And when is this dance?" Hugh asked.

"This Saturday."

"That's in only a week. I knew you liked her when I saw you at church this Sunday. The way you stared at her while the circuit preacher delivered such a moving sermon. I mean to have a discussion with him about it when I see him next. To think of the victories God gave a shepherd boy, taking him from among the sheepfold and transforming him into a great king. There I was, completely immersed in the key points, and I happened to catch you staring away at a lovely girl on the pew across the aisle."

Jake chuckled. "I suppose you have caught me. Maybe you'll see the preacher at the dance."

"Maybe I will," Hugh said as another knock interrupted them.

Brent Tolliver stepped inside the library and bowed slightly. "I'm sorry to disturb you, sir, but you have another visitor."

Jake rolled his eyes. "Here we go again. Every businessman in town has been to my door this week. Who is it this time?"

"Mr. Chip Greer, the brother of Miss Adelaide Greer of Miss Adelaide's Jam Company, sir," Tolliver replied.

"And does he also come asking me to run for mayor?" Jake asked. "Or is he asking to buy the extra town lots like the Keller fellow, the gold prospector?"

"I'm afraid he didn't want to state his business," Tolliver answered.

Hugh chuckled. "I think it's marvelous. You should run for mayor, Jake. This town loved your grandfather. They want you to carry on the tradition. Whatever you do, don't sell the town lots to that Keller fellow. I don't trust him any."

"I don't have any intention of selling the extra vacant town lots to a prospector, but I am not my grandfather, and I haven't a clue what makes a good mayor. I've been trying to figure it all out from reading my grandfather's notes and letters, pouring over his ledgers, but I'm not sure I have any idea of what a truly good mayor should do." Jake glanced at Tolliver, still waiting for his direction. He sighed. "Go ahead. Show this Chip Greer inside."

"Very good, sir," Tolliver replied.

"Well, how's it going?" Mrs. Penworth asked as she arranged another tea tray. "Is it working?"

Tolliver shrugged as he reached for one of Mrs. Penworth's warm scones. "I'm not entirely sure."

"Who's in the library with Master Hunter now?" she inquired, adding a sugar bowl to the tray.

Tolliver tasted some of the scone and closed his eyes as he chewed. "These are delicious, Mrs. Penworth. This time it's Sheldon Thornton, the owner of the Honey River Gazette. Yesterday, he tried to approach Master Hunter when he visited the trading post to look over the ledger there, and Master would have none of it. Zeb Thompson and Edwin Winters are waiting for their turns in the great hall. None of them want to see one of the Martins become our mayor, and they all say they prefer the colonel's grandson."

"The colonel didn't like anyone bothering him either when he looked over the books at the Bradshaw Trading Post. He was very particular about not being disturbed when he had impor-tant work to do, and he liked to stay on task," the housekeeper replied. "It seems like our plan is working so far. Between my Arthur, you, and Clifton Danvers, I think we've managed to visit a great many who would likely vote for Jacob. Now all we have to do is let it simmer until he realizes he has plenty of town support."

"Yes, and from many of the area farmers, too." Tolliver nodded. "We've had our share of them calling on him. I don't know if Chad Martin has enough support to win since Jacob Hunter has arrived."

Mrs. Penworth smiled and handed him the tea tray. She smoothed the folds in her long black skirt. "Time will tell. It's all ready for you to take to the library to serve master's guests. I've added extra cups so you don't have to keep returning to the kitchen as often."

Tolliver grinned and straightened his black short-waisted coat. "Thank you for thinking of my feet, Mrs. Penworth. You're a real gem around here."

Mrs. Penworth pressed her lips together in a guarded smile, but evidence of her appreciation caused her eyes to sparkle in response. "For that, you may have an extra scone."

Chapter Ten

The heart of the discerning acquires knowledge, for the ears of the wise seek it out.

Proverbs 18:15, NIV

"May I give you a ride, Josie? I'm guessing you're on your way to St. Paul's Mission." Chad Martin pulled his buggy to a stop on the side of Honey Avenue where Josie walked. She'd cut straight down Third Street through town, and now she only had just under about a mile to walk to reach Bell Avenue where the mission sat on the far southwestern corner of town. Bell Avenue intersected with Honey Avenue and Fourth Street at a sharp angle, and the mission, situated parallel to Bell, faced the town at the same sharp angle. She supposed they'd named it Bell Avenue because of the mission bell hanging in the tower above the nave. She could have taken the wagon or ridden Mrs. Velvet, or one of their other horses, but she'd chosen to walk in order to take in the fresh air and lovely scenery. After being cooped up in the cabin all winter, it felt good to be outside, and the exercise didn't harm her any, either.

Josie squinted in the sunlight as she looked up at Chad, surprised to find him heading south. "Yes, I am on my way to the mission. What brings you out here all this way?"

"I'm on my way to the Nelson farm to make sure I can count on Mac's vote."

"Oh, I see. Well, his farm is located beside the mission. I guess I'll ride with you since you're going that way." She stepped around toward the passenger seat of the buggy as he jumped down to help her inside.

"Good, because there's a few things I wanted to ask you." He handed her up into the buggy and Josie settled into the seat, spreading out the folds of her calico day dress.

Returning to the driver's seat, he released the brake and snapped the reins on his horse. The buggy moved forward as she pulled her shawl closer around her shoulders. "I heard you're running for mayor."

He smiled and nodded. "I am, and I hope I can count on you to stand by my side."

"Stand by your side?" she repeated, tucking a stray strand of hair into the chignon under her bonnet.

Chad nodded. "Josie, we've known each other a mighty long time, haven't we?"

Reluctant to answer, she looked out onto a prairie meadow to their left. "We have."

"I know I've asked you before, but I won't ask again. I could make life easier for you, Josie. We could be married. You wouldn't have to work so hard to make Cherry Crossing the farm you want it to be. I'd take care of everything you need, and I'd be a good husband to you, Josie."

She gulped, biting her lower lip.

"And I wanted to ask you to the dance," he added.

When she didn't say anything, he continued. "The Martin spread would be the largest farm in Honey River Canyon if we marry. You'd be set for life, married to the new mayor, assuming I win the election, of course. You do know one day I'll inherit everything my pa owns. You'd never have to worry about plowing and planting ever again, and we could work something out for the care of your sisters. You could come and live with us after we're wed, and my sisters and Ma would be so happy to have you there."

Josie thought about his sisters, Hope and Joy, and their younger brother, Samuel, and his sweet roping tricks he learned from his older brothers. She didn't know what Chad meant exactly about working out something for the care of her sisters, but she suspected they'd not be invited to live in the grand farmhouse the Martins had on account of being the wealthiest cattle farmers in the region. She sighed, remembering Pa had warned her the Martins wanted to absorb Cherry Crossing. What would become of them if she married him? What would become of Cherry Crossing? Something inside her didn't trust him or his family to let her make decisions concerning the farmstead after a marriage to Chad. She also didn't believe Chad truly loved her as much as he loved his family and the cattle ranch he'd inherit one day. She knew she didn't love Chad, but she didn't know how long she'd known she didn't love him.

Turning to him, she decided the time had come to set him free. "Chad, you know I think the world of you. We've been good friends all these years, and it's not that I don't appreciate all you've done for us, helping us with the plowing and planting and harvesting since the passing of my parents, but I think you should move on and marry someone for love. I'd only feel like a business transaction if we married, and as for the dance, I've previously agreed to attend with someone else."

"You have?" he asked, pulling the reins tight. "Whoa, boy! Whoa!" Once the buggy had stopped, he turned and looked into her eyes, removing his hat.

"I think you've got the wrong idea, Josie," he began. "I've always loved you, ever since the first day I saw you. I thought you knew that when I brought marriage up after your folks passed away."

"That was nearly six years ago, and I suppose I have always known it, but as much as I care for you as a very good and dear friend and neighbor, Chad Martin, I will never marry you. I confess I have thought about your offer a thousand times, but I know deep in my heart it will never work."

"Why didn't you tell me before now?" He shifted in his seat, shaking his head.

"For one thing, I needed to prove to myself I could handle things at Cherry Crossing, and if one or more of my sisters and I never marry, it will always remain a home for any of us who may need it. Pa and Ma left the farmstead to the three of us in equal part, you see. The Martins should not have anything to do with our decisions regarding it, even if we married. It belongs to my sisters and me. For another thing, even though you profess your love to me, I cannot profess to return it, but I don't think I knew it of a certainty until recently."

Chad raked a hand through his hair, absorbing all she said. "I see ... I guess I'm just surprised to hear all of this."

"I know, but I am trying to set things straight with you. Chad, you are free to pursue any girl you like. I'll always consider you a close friend who is dear to my heart. You and your brother have helped us tremendously, and I'll never forget it."

His mouth hung open, but he closed it, opened it again, and then closed it. Looking away, he snapped the reins. "I guess it's settled then. We're just friends from here on out."

She nodded, pulling her shawl tighter, hoping he would finally move on with his life. It didn't seem fair to keep him waiting in the wings in case she ever changed her mind. She'd tried to tell him before, but he hadn't listened. This time, it sounded as though he'd finally understood. She made a few attempts at small talk about the weather, the mission, and the price of wheat as they continued the journey across Honey River Canyon, but relief flooded her when he pulled into the circular drive at St. Paul's Mission. She jumped down from the buggy the moment it came to a stop, thanked him for the ride, and hurried inside. *Dear Lord, please don't let Chad Martin be sorrowful over me, nor vindictive about this.*

Chapter Eleven

Carry each other's burdens, and in this way, you will fulfill the law of Christ.

Galatians 6:2, NIV

Once inside the mission, Josie closed her eyes and thanked the Lord for the relatively calm response she'd received from Chad. A handsome man, releasing him could end up a mistake, but she had never found herself able to commit to the relationship on any level other than friendship. Coming to terms with clearly letting him go only made sense. Sure, his presence seemed convenient and reassuring at times, like a kind of safety net, but she couldn't keep putting him off knowing deep down she didn't truly love him.

This, she had known for some time, and perhaps it had

taken the passion between her and the colonel's grandson to know with complete certainty she wanted something more. Josie desired a marriage of love, something deeper than what she'd felt when Chad had kissed her at the creek three times, and in the barn loft twice. He had certainly never caused her to feel like Jake Hunter had when he'd kissed her, and now she knew letting Chad go to pursue Jake with a full heart made perfect sense.

Nonetheless, Jake wasn't off the hook yet from buying her horse out from under her. Sometimes when she thought about it, she wanted to create a much bigger fuss than she had thus far, but her faith in God and other ideals held her back when she very much wanted to lose her temper.

Josie walked down the main hall and entered the dining hall on her right, heading across the large room toward the kitchen on the other end, hoping to find Mother Marta. Marta always had a kind word for her and the most loving, bright blue eyes. She would smile at her and in those moments, Josie knew everything would turn out exactly as it should, somehow reassured of the fact the Lord would never forsake her. "Have courage, my dear," Mother Marta would say. "Have faith and courage in the Lord. He is always faithful. He never leaves us."

The mission had an arrangement with Josie to come and work whenever she could for seventy-five cents per day. She helped with the cooking, laundry, cleaning, giving French lessons, and other light tasks they assigned her. Sometimes they'd ask her to grade papers, help with lesson planning, read to the children, tend the kitchen garden, or any number of other tasks. Although Josie considered herself a Protestant Congregationalist, working at a Catholic mission didn't cause any conflict regarding her faith. She figured they both believed in Jesus, and this main important belief connected her to the wonderful people at the mission.

Her mind wrestled with her thoughts, wondering if she would regret her decision by letting Chad go, and if she could truly give Jake a fair chance after what had happened with Blue. Distracted by her thoughts, she ran right into Sister Angel. The two collided, and Josie realized the nun carried a book of prayers, reading from it while she walked. At the same time, she carried a metal bowl of garden peas against one hip, but the bowl dislodged, made a great clanking, and the peas flew everywhere.

"Oh, I'm so sorry, Sister Angel." Josie bent down at once, scrambling to pick up the peas as the metal bowl continued to make noise as it spun on the stone floor. "It's my fault entirely. I wasn't looking where I was going."

The nun closed her book and tucked it under her arm. She knelt in her black habit to assist with retrieving the scattered peas. "'Tis no problem, Miss Hayes. I shouldn't have been reading and walking at the same time. I must say, I'm happy to see you. The children have missed you. They'll be so happy you're here."

"Would you like me to shell the peas for you?" Josie asked as they gathered up the pods. "What has happened to your eyeglasses, Sister Angel?"

"Certainly, if you'd like to, it will help us a great deal. Sister Agnes usually does it as you know, but she is suffering so much of late. I am trying to help Sister Francesca by setting the tables in here for lunch, but I was going to shell the peas first." Sister Angel explained as the children's voices echoed into the hall from the large chapel where they studied their lessons each day. Every now and then, Josie could hear Padre Cornelius recite a line from Psalm ninety-one. Then the children would repeat the line in unison. "As for my eyeglasses, they fell, and one spectacle cracked, and now I can only see out of one eye."

"Oh dear. I'm sorry to hear about your spectacles. I'm also sorry to hear about Sister Agnes. How is everyone else? How is Mother Marta? Is she well? And Bishop Thomas? Is he doing well?" Josie inquired, knowing Sister Agnes, partially deaf and quite elderly, had frequent bouts of bad days and poor health at times.

Sister Angel scooped up the last few peas and dropped them inside the metal bowl. "The rest of us are in good health, although I should take a cup of tea and some broth upstairs to Sister Agnes. Mother Marta went into town to buy some supplies, but she should be returning soon. Bishop Thomas had a cold for a few days, but he has greatly improved."

"'Tis a good idea to take some refreshment to Sister Agnes. She struggles so with her health. How is Robin? Is her spelling and reading improving?" Josie tried not to have favorite students since she loved them all, but the sweet little orphan girl had always clung to her. She'd spent a great deal of time trying to help the little Indian girl improve her English and grammar skills. Padre Cornelius had bequeathed Robin and her sister, Star, with unique Christian names upon their arrival at the mission when they'd become separated from their tribe after sickness had stolen the lives of their parents. They'd been toddlers then, but now they were ages ten and twelve.

"Robin is doing very well, but she will be so happy to see you, Miss Hayes. Sister Agnes is resting today and won't be downstairs to help us at all. She has some aches and pain in her joints, and the winter has been hard on her this year, as you know."

"I'm so sorry to hear about Sister Agnes. I wish there was something else we could do for her. I brought some ribbons for Star and Robin's hair, and I can't wait to see them."

"The girls will be thrilled." On this note, the nun smiled and returned to the kitchen to retrieve bowls, plates, and utensils. Josie sat down at one of the long, empty tables to shell the peas, easing into her workday.

As she finished the task, Mother Marta burst through the door with some brown paper packages in her arms. "You'll never guess the news I've had today, sisters," she called out, stopping in her tracks when she saw Josie. "Jocelyn! Is that you? How nice to see you. Guess who's running for mayor, everyone."

"I have no idea," Josie replied, her eyes lighting up to see the Mother Superior.

Sister Francesca poked her head around the corner from the kitchen and placed her hands on her hips over her black habit. "Did you say someone is running for mayor?"

Sister Angel replied for Marta with a nod as she finished setting the children's tables for lunch. "Aye, she did."

"Colonel Bradshaw's grandson, a Mr. Jacob Hunter, has arrived from Pennsylvania, and he is continuing the tradition of his grandfather by running for mayor. He goes by Jake, but doesn't Mayor Hunter have a nice ring to it, sisters?" Marta stood still in the dining hall for a moment with her arms full as she shared the news.

"Interesting news indeed," Sister Angel commented.

Mother Marta continued. "And, Chad Martin is running, too. It was just announced today according to Katy and Clark Emmerson. My guess is Josie here knows since they're neighbors, and the Martins have always helped at Cherry Crossing."

"I did hear about Chad, initially from my sister, but I didn't know about Jake, although we suspected he would run, being the colonel's grandson." Josie smiled with the others at hearing the tidings, but she also wondered if Chad Martin would become enemies to his opponent. She pushed the concern aside and rose to her feet to assist Marta with her armful of goods. "Mayor Hunter does have a nice ring, indeed. Let me help you with those packages. I have missed you all so much. We've been so busy with the spring planting; I haven't been able to come."

"First tell me, did you get the horse you wanted?" Marta transferred some of her packages into Josie's arms and they walked toward the kitchen from the dining hall together.

She shook her head. "No. It's a long, dreadful story. We're still looking, sadly."

The nun turned to her after they'd reached the worktable in the kitchen and set the items down. "I'm so sorry, Josie. I know how much the horse meant to you and how hard you worked for it. What a terrible disappointment this must have been for you."

Josie nodded. "Thank you. We'll find another."

"Of course, you will. God always provides, dear." Mother Marta set about helping in the kitchen by putting away the items she'd purchased in town. Then she joined Sister Francesca and Sister Angel by rolling up her sleeves, washing her hands, and then chopping a bowl of turnips. Josie, finished with shelling the peas, began peeling some carrots.

"We'll have mashed turnips for our supper with the peas and carrots on the side. I've been simmering some chicken broth and cream for the turnips. If we remember to add two or three chopped potatoes, together with the sweetness in the cream, it will help take the bitterness out of the largest turnips," Sister Francesca explained to Josie as she began sorting through a bowl of salad greens from the garden. "These will be for our lunch, along with the applesauce, the cornbread squares, and some chicken broth. I know the broth isn't much, but it's what the Lord has provided."

"It sounds like a fine meal to me. Ma always said a heavy noonday meal isn't good for proper digestion." Josie chopped the ends off a carrot. "The way you prepare turnips is the way my ma prepared them, too. She always added the cream and a potato to sweeten them."

"I'm guessing you miss her very much," Mother Marta commented. "I miss my Ma, too. We never really recover from losing our loved ones, but I remind myself I'll see her again one day by staying close to the Lord."

"I wish I had known my mother. Like some of these orphans, I never had the opportunity, but the Lord has stayed near to my side. I've always felt His presence watching over me, comforting me, guiding me." Angel picked up the pan of broth by the handle with a folded cloth and headed toward the dining hall with a ladle in her other hand. "I'm ready to ladle the broth into the bowls. I shall return."

"I can't imagine not having known my parents. It makes me thankful for the time the Lord gave my sisters and me with them. They taught us so much and loved us so faithfully. I'm glad for the memories I have of my parents." Josie used the paring knife to peel a thin strip of the outer skin from the carrot in her hands, careful not to waste any of the vegetable.

"That is exactly the right attitude, Jocelyn. Don't dwell on the negative aspects," Marta replied, still chopping turnips at the other end of the worktable where Josie stood. "Those who remain positive in life and make the best of difficult situations will become victorious over life's challenges. We can take note from the Israelites who grumbled in the wilderness. Grumbling never gets us anywhere except in circles, an endless cycle of destruction."

"I have come to the same conclusion, and thankfully, my sisters and I have not fallen into the trap of complaining. God has given us a good life, all things considered. It's what we make of our opportunities, like you said, Mother Marta. I wake up each day and thank the Lord for another day to serve Him. I am choosing to focus on the joy in life and being thankful for what we have. What would you like me to do after lunch has been served, sisters?" Josie asked. In truth, on some days, feeling thankful did not come easy to her, but she tried to overcome. Sometimes she indulged in self-pity, but somehow, the Holy Spirit helped her navigate toward thinking positive thoughts in those times. Self-pity tended to result in a wasteland leading nowhere, and she didn't like to spend time on that road.

Marta smiled as she scooped the chopped parsnips into a large bowl, setting it aside to add to the stock later. "You are wise beyond your years, Miss Josie. Would you mind helping us with the washing? The linens have been stripped from the children's beds upstairs, but they need laundered and hung on the line. After the noonday meal, I can put fresh linens on the beds, and Sister Angel can teach the children their mathematics, and

Sister Francesca can wash the dishes. Then we can have tea at three o'clock with Bishop Thomas and Padre Cornelius. Maybe Sister Agnes will join us."

Josie nodded, knowing in advance, it meant boiling the linens in a large kettle of water over a campfire outside. She would stir two or three of the linens at a time with a long stick, adding lye to the water, and stirring until soap suds appeared. Then, using the stick, she'd transfer the linens one at a time to a bucket of cool well water for rinsing. She would need to change out this water for fresh water whenever it didn't look clear of suds.

The task required strength and patience, especially since wringing the sheets out before hanging them to dry involved twisting and squeezing. These did not come easy to her, but she knew the nuns struggled even more with the task. "Certainly. I'm happy to do it. I'll enjoy the fresh air and sunshine. I'm sure the children will come and say hello during their recess after lunch."

"Of course, they will. They'll be so happy to see you." Sister Francesca smiled. "They've been asking about you."

Josie smiled to hear this. True to Sister Francesca's words, the children came to say hello to her numerous times while she worked outside behind the mission at the area appointed for laundry. Robin came running to her first, her braids flying out behind her as she ran to her side. She raced straight through the chickens, and clucking, they parted like the Red Sea.

"Miss Hayes! Miss Hayes!" Catching up to her, Robin flung her arms around Josie's waist. "I missed you so much."

Josie bent down and smiled, patting the ten-year-old orphan. "I missed you too, but I brought you something."

"You did?" Robin's eyes widened.

"You must tell the others I had a little extra of what's inside this and gave you some, but they are brand new, except it's our little secret," Josie said, reaching in her hidden skirt pocket to withdraw a small package.

Robin nodded eagerly, tearing the package open to reveal the pink satin ribbons. Her face lit up, and she ran her fingers along the smooth fabric, smiling. "Thank you. I love them."

"Let me put them in your hair for you." Josie tied the ribbons in each of her braids. Reaching in her pocket again, she produced a second package. "These are for Star, your sister. They are blue so you won't mix them up. You must give them to her when no one is looking."

Robin nodded, reaching up to feel the new ribbons in her hair. "Thank you, Miss Hayes. I love them. I will give these to my sister when no one is looking."

"Very good. Run along and play, and we'll talk again before I go if there is time," Josie instructed as Anna and Helena, the eldest female students, approached.

"All right. I'll be sitting over there on the log playing with my ragdoll, Luisa." Robin smiled and ran to the log laying on the ground where she could sit, playing with her doll, and yet remain near to Josie.

Anna and Helena said hello and offered a hand with the linens. Then Ava, Edwina, and Rachel came to greet her. Star and Christy came next. After they'd caught Josie up on all the news about their studies and happenings around the mission, they joined Robin to sit on the log with their rag dolls. Next came the four boys, Joel, Peter, Stephen, and Christopher. They lingered around the campfire, offering to bring more logs whenever she needed them. When Mother Marta stepped outside to ring a small handbell signifying the end of recess, the children returned to the classroom in the chapel for their afternoon lessons. Robin waved to her again, and Josie returned the wave before the little girl followed the others inside.

When she finished washing the linens, Josie returned inside the mission, comprised of two wings shaped like an "L." The chapel and nave, located below the bell tower in the middle where the wings joined, emptied at precisely three o'clock each afternoon for tea. One wing housed Padre Cornelius, Bishop Thomas, and the four orphan boys schooled at the mission. The other housed the dining hall, the kitchen, the great parlor, and above these, rooms for the nuns and female students.

Sister Francesca passed out apples and biscuits to the children. Then they went outside with their treats to play while the adults gathered around the fireplace in the great parlor for tea.

"Good afternoon, Miss Hayes," Padre Cornelius said in his Irish brogue once they had all settled in the room on the various wooden pews used as parlor benches or one of several rocking chairs. "'Tis nice to see you. I'm guessing you have been busy with spring planting as we have been here at the mission?"

Josie nodded. "Yes, Padre Cornelius, I have. My sisters and I are looking forward to the dance this Saturday, as well. Perhaps we will see all of you there."

An uncomfortable silence filled the room, and Josie wondered what she had said to cause it as they looked down and sipped their tea. She didn't sip her tea, but instead studied them. None looked her in the eye except Mother Marta.

"What? Don't tell me you won't be attending the spring dance?" Shocked, Josie returned Marta's pensive gaze, hoping she'd provide an answer and break the uncomfortable silence. It occurred to Josie just then as she waited for a reply, she'd never seen the orphans, nuns, or anyone from the mission in attendance at any of the community dances.

"We have not attended any of the dances before," Mother Marta said in a soft voice.

This fact surprised Josie. "Oh, I do hope you'll change your mind. I think it would be most beneficial to the children. Not only for the children, but for the mission to unite with the community."

Padre Cornelius leaned his head to one side as he considered her statement. Mother Marta sipped some of her tea with a brief glance at him before she turned back with a soft reply to Jocelyn. "Perhaps you are right, Miss Josie. Maybe it is time to reconsider the mission's position on attending community dances."

Josie didn't speak about the dance anymore after this. Instead, she sipped her tea quietly as Sister Angel turned the conversation to how nicely the mission's kitchen garden progressed as she began to make mention of each of the vegetables and herbs they'd planted. On her next visit, Josie would teach another French lesson to the children in the afternoon before Sister Agnes instructed the children in either a sewing or art class if her health improved. With this established, Josie said farewell when she'd finished her tea and headed outside for the walk home, saddened the children had never known the joy of attending a community dance.

Chapter Twelve

I will greatly rejoice in the Lord, my soul shall be joyful in my God; for He hath clothed me with the garments of salvation, He hath covered me with the robe of righteousness, as a bridegroom decketh himself with ornaments, and as a bride adorneth herself with her jewels.

Isaiah 61:10

Friday morning, Josie rode Violet to town on her way to the mission. As she held the reins steady, she took in the signs of late spring and the approach of summer all around. Colorful yellow blanket flowers with their reddish orange centers sprawled across a grassy meadow, reminding her of daisies with their bursts of pineleaf blooms on small shrubs with their needle-like leaves. Occasional purple Rocky Mountain spikes atop evergreen foliage dotted the side of the road, and bright pink cone-flowers crept up in meadows, drawing birds and bees to drink their nectar.

She had taken a shortcut to town by cutting across Cherry Crossing toward the base of Silver Mountain. The closer she drew, the greener it appeared, but from the cabin, the mountain always looked gray and silvery like rock, hence its name. She steered the horse along beside the base of winding mountains towering up on her left, continuing toward the area where the town of Honey River Canyon emerged, past Blue Sapphire Mountain, positioned slightly behind Silver Mountain. Then she passed Pearl Mountain and Black Onyx Mountain. She could see Honey River in the distance when pines and other trees didn't block her view, but after Honey Mountain, the river disappeared behind Emerald Mountain and Jade Mountain, then reappearing as it curved around in front of the base of Gold Mountain.

Across from Gold Mountain, Josie had a choice to steer the horse onto the northern end of Fourth Street, or continue through the countryside, cutting across meadows and around wooded areas as she neared Canyon Lake. This would take her to Bell Avenue and the mission, but she would have to cut across untamed land beyond the mayor's mansion. She chose the latter and urged Violet into a steady gallop.

She urged Violet to go faster as they approached Honey Creek, giving her horse plenty of speed to jump over the narrowest part of the creek. They flew over it without any trouble, but immediately after the broodmare landed on the other side, Josie heard a long whistle from behind them. This caused her to pull in the reins a little as she looked over her shoulder, slowing Violet to a trot. Catching sight of Jake astride a horse she didn't recognize, she gave the command for her mount to stop. "Whoa! Whoa, girl." Then she turned Violet around to their left, steering the horse toward Jake as his horse craned his long neck and mane after drinking from the creek to have a look at them.

"Hello, Jake," she said. "How nice to see you." *Good Josie. The first truly civil words you've ever spoken to the man.*

Jake tipped his hat in her direction. "That was a nice jump, and it's a pleasure to see you, too."

"Thank you," she replied, patting Violet for her fine foot-work and smooth landing.

"I was going to ride out to ask you a question this morning, but here you are…" He turned his horse toward hers and drew closer, both of them coming to a stop beside each other.

"Yes, here I am," she replied. "Ask away…"

"I was going to ask if you would mind if my friend, Hugh Stanton, came along with us to the dance, perhaps as an escort for one of your sisters or another friend. I'm guessing your sisters may already have accepted escorts, but maybe you can recommend someone he could pair with, purely as friends, of course. He is engaged to wed in late June."

"Ah. May I ask, to clarify, are you referring to the friend who drove his wagon like a wild man through town?" One of her brows shot up as she waited on his answer.

He nodded. "That's the one. Of course, if you prefer other-wise, then I won't bring him along, and he can meet us at the event of his own accord."

Tilting her head, Josie considered the matter. "My youngest sister might not be opposed to the idea. She is studying to become a teacher, and consequently, courting is not high on her list of priorities at present. She had every intention of attending the dance independent of any beau, but I think she would be pleased if Hugh would be her escort for the evening."

"Very good then. We'll pick you ladies up in the carriage." Jake winked at her and tipped his hat again.

"I am looking forward to it, Jake Hunter."

"See you then, Miss Hayes." Jake steered his horse toward the mansion, and Josie turned Violet toward the mission, a smile on her face at having seen the handsome Mr. Hunter again.

After Josie's French class, she sat with Mother Marta at the teacher's table in the dining hall organizing some glass and ceramic beads and colorful threads donated to the mission for the children to use in various projects. With the beads spread out before them on one end of the table, they separated them by color, placing them into glass bowls. Sister Agnes's voice occasionally drifted from across the hall as the nun taught the children how to sketch a landscape. Her health had improved and on this particular afternoon, she sounded even a tad jovial and sprightly.

In French class, since a few weeks had passed since Josie had instructed them, she had focused on leading the children through a series of oral exercises and repetition of French phrases of greetings, partings, and light conversation such as "Bonjour," "Au revoir," and "Je m'appelle Mademoiselle Josie," which made them laugh.

She credited her mother for teaching her French since Ma had learned to speak, read, and write it while attending a finishing school in St. Paul which taught ladies proper etiquette. In fact, she still used Ma's French books for teaching the language. Sometimes she opened the books to stare at the penned maiden name of her Ma, Rose Johnson, carefully written in cursive on the inside cover to designate ownership. Though Ma's signature had faded a little, the handwriting and books somehow comforted her, keeping her connected to her mother, just as Ma's collection of McGuffey Readers did. She had a feeling her mother would approve of her work as a teacher and employee at St. Paul's Mission.

"Did someone special ask you to the dance, Miss Josie?" the Mother Superior asked, one brow rising in curiosity. "I know it's tomorrow. You and your sisters must be looking forward to it."

Josie smiled and looked down at the beads, thinking how lovely some of the pearly ones would look if sewn onto a bodice, and acknowledging to herself it did not sound as if the staff at the mission had decided in favor of attending the event. "Jake Hunter has asked to escort me to the dance, and yes, we are very much looking forward to it."

"He is a very handsome gentleman. Did you know I had a conversation with him yesterday when I went into town to pick up our order of jam from Miss Adelaide's?"

"You did?" Josie looked up in surprise.

Mother Marta nodded and concentrated on separating some pale blue beads from some pale pink ones. "He was an assistant pastor for four years in Philadelphia, but he asked me not to divulge this to the general population of Honey River

Canyon, but as you are not the general population, and you don't participate in gossip, I thought you should know."

Would wonders ever cease? What else did she not know about Jake Hunter? "Thank you for sharing this with me. I didn't know." Josie continued to gather the pearly looking beads. "Have you had a moment to speak with Padre Cornelius about taking the children to the dance?"

"We did talk more about it, in fact. We had a chat in the great parlor last night by the fire while toasting some slices of bread and cheese on sticks in the fireplace. It was fun and delicious, but we have decided to stick with our policy... much to the disappointment of our students."

"I'm deeply sorry to hear this, but I understand." Josie took particular care not to sigh about the decision. She did her best to remain respectful concerning the matter.

"Sister Francesca is hopeful," Mother Marta confided, "but I didn't mention it if anyone asks."

"I won't mention it." Josie closed her eyes and made the sign of the cross over herself. She could not help but smile about the remark. It meant hope existed. Perhaps the policy would change in time.

Her actions made Marta laugh. "I would venture to guess you are praying the policy will change or that you do not divulge Sister Francesca's hopes, or both. I pray you and Mr. Jake Hunter have a wonderful time at the dance."

"Thank you, Mother Marta. Yes, I'm praying for both. I hope we have a nice time at the dance, too. I encountered him out riding this morning on my way to the mission, and he said he'd bring his friend Hugh along as an escort for my younger sister. They are going to the dance as friends since he is engaged to someone else."

"And who is your middle sister going with? Jacqueline is her name, yes?"

Josie nodded. "Yes. Jackie is going with a fellow who's new in town, Abel Keller. Don't ask me anything else. I don't know anything yet except he and his brother, Cadence, are gold prospectors. Cadence's wife, Florence, has taken my sister under her wing as a friend, and I guess they are loaded."

"Loaded?" Mother Marta's brow furrowed at this expression, and a curious look appeared in her eyes.

"Rich. And it's Jackie's greatest dream to marry above our station in life, so nothing I could ever say will stop them from being together."

"Ah. I see. I shall pray for Jacqueline. I shall also pray your youngest sister and the engaged friend do not fall into a dangerous love affair."

Josie's mouth dropped open. She made the sign of the cross over herself again. "Have you been reading too many romance novels, Mother Marta?"

Marta laughed, and Josie with her. "Maybe."

When their chuckles subsided, Josie confessed, "In truth, I hadn't considered the possibility since Jackie's new romantic interest consumes most of my worries. Jillian is very sensible and determined to become a teacher. She generally gives me little cause for concern. However, I must thank you. Your prayers mean a great deal to me, and one never knows when it comes to matters of the heart how things can escalate."

"Indeed." Mother Marta dropped a few more pink beads into a bowl. "I haven't given up on persuading Padre Cornelius about the benefits of participating in more community events, but I think it may take some time to convince him, and I am not entirely convinced myself for a number of reasons. In any case, you might have a word with Robin this afternoon. I caught her sulking yesterday evening. When I asked her what was wrong, she said she is sad she will not get to attend the dance because she wanted to sit beside you and learn to dance."

"Oh, I had no idea. She is such a sweet child. I will have a word with her before I leave."

The evening of the spring dance finally arrived, and the Hayes sisters hurried to ready themselves. They each took turns taking a bath behind a screen in the kitchen, towel drying their long hair, and putting on their best frocks over their prettiest lace-trimmed petticoats. Jacqueline shared her perfume consisting of bergamot and jasmine with a hint of orange. They dotted their wrists, hair, and behind their ears with the fragrance.

Josie pulled on a burgundy, empire-waisted dress with a square neckline before winding her dark brown hair into a fancy updo and pinning it in place. The long sleeves of her dress would keep her warm on a cool spring evening. She'd add a navy shawl, white gloves, and a simple straw bonnet lined in navy to match the shawl to complete her look.

"Have you seen my best stockings, Jill?" Jackie's voice called out from her bedroom.

"No idea," returned Jill's answer.

"Can I borrow some of yours?" Jackie asked, sounding aggravated, creating a ruckus in the background as it sounded like she might be crawling about on all fours and tossing things about in a mad search for the stockings, looking under all things.

A creak sounded as a door opened. "I'm tossing them out into the hall," Jill answered before her door firmly closed again.

Josie did her best to ignore the stream of calamities happening in their cozy cabin as she fished through Ma's meager collection of jewelry. She enjoyed looking at each of the treasures in the small cedar box on the bureau in her parents' bedroom until she found the item she wanted to borrow from the box, Ma's genuine pearl necklace with the pretty clasp. Jacqueline had asked if she could wear Ma's gold locket necklace with the blue ruffled dress with the lovely bustle she'd decided to wear, and Jillian wanted to wear Ma's brooch with her favorite high-collared white blouse, a lavender shawl, and dark purple skirt. At least they would each have something from their mother to wear to the dance.

After she secured the clasp on the necklace and added the shawl, Josie stood back to check her appearance in Ma's full-length oval mirror positioned in one corner of the room. Though it now functioned as a guest bedroom, she and her sisters had decided years ago to keep everything exactly as Ma and Pa had kept it. The same quilt with violet roses and butter-flies stitched into the pattern and down-feathered pillows still graced the bed. Sometimes she could almost smell Ma's rose-water scented perfume lingering in her pillow and in the room. Ma's hope chest still sat at the footboard Pa had carved to match the headboard, a gift he'd given Ma for their wedding.

They'd brought the bed west to Montana Territory from Minnesota. Rose Elizabeth Johnson had become his mail-order bride after he'd placed an ad in a St. Paul newspaper. She'd responded to the advertisement, and Nathaniel Edward Hayes and Rose Elizabeth Johnson had married in St. Paul after exchanging a few letters. Her parents and one brother, Uncle Edwin, had attended the ceremony, but their romance blossomed in Pa's hometown of Duluth after their private church wedding. Pa brought her ma home to his father's farm located in a rural area of the Lake Superior port city, not far from a place Josie remembered called Gooseberry Falls.

She and her sisters were each born there, but when Jocelyn turned eight, they'd packed up a few of their most treasured possessions and moved their three daughters west in a covered wagon to claim their own land in Montana Territory in response to the 1862 Homestead Act. Now her paternal Aunt Louisa and her husband kept the farm running in Duluth, and her maternal Uncle Edwin and his wife ran a general store in St. Paul. She hadn't seen any of them in fifteen years, and longer for her St. Paul relations. Her grandparents had all passed on, but some cousins had been born whom she'd never met. She didn't plan on running to them for help if she and her sisters could continue to thrive at Cherry Crossing in Honey River Canyon.

Pa had imported cherry trees from Canada and planted a small orchard. He'd also planted an apple orchard. He plowed fields for wheat, potatoes, and corn. Though Nathaniel and Rose had barely known each other when they'd married, their love had grown into something fierce and timeless. Josie ran her fingers over the pretty necklace, another gift Pa had given her ma for an anniversary gift one year. Ma had treasured the pearls because Pa had worked hard to afford real ones, but she had occasionally enjoyed faux jewelry and other little trinkets.

Josie couldn't help but wonder if she would ever find a love like theirs as she placed the finishing touches on her appearance. She also wondered if she would regret stepping out with Jake—a man she'd called a scoundrel and a swindler, as he'd been quick to point out the day he'd knocked her down in his rather clumsy attempt to protect her from a stray bullet. She'd find out soon enough since Ma's mantel clock downstairs ticked the seconds away as it grew closer to chiming seven o'clock. At any moment, Jake Hunter, Hugh Stanton, and Abel Keller would arrive.

Chapter Thirteen

Trust in the Lord with all thine heart; and lean not unto thine own understanding. In all thy ways acknowledge Him, and He shall direct thy paths.

Proverbs 3:5-6

Abel Keller, with Cadence and Florence Keller seated in a carriage for four, arrived first, twenty-three minutes early. Jill and Josie waved from the front door as he helped their middle sister into her seat. Josie couldn't help but bite her lower lip as she observed them drive away. She guessed the Keller brothers had rented the conveyance from the livery and hired a recommended driver she recognized as one of the local farm boys. Shortly after they turned onto the lane leading to town, Hugh and Jake arrived in similar fashion. Ollie Campbell, one of

Jake's grandfather's stable hands, drove the foursome to the town hall in style equivalent to one of the livery's finest rented carriages. The colonel had always maintained the very best of everything.

Josie smiled to see Jake and Hugh holding a bouquet of flowers for each of them when she opened the door. "Hello," she said, accepting the flowers Jake handed her. "These are beautiful. You remembered! I see everything in this lovely bouquet. Buttercups, sweet pea, larkspur, yellow bells, geraniums, shooting stars, *and* hyacinths! I have no idea how you managed this, Jake. Especially the hyacinths. Ours never bloom for long."

Hugh shook his head, his eyes growing big as he evidently remembered a challenging couple of days. He chuckled and a wide grin appeared on his face as Jill joined them at the door and he handed her a similar bunch of flowers. "He's been plucking flowers from behind the mansion, in the meadows, and gardens about town for days," Hugh shared, giving his friend a sideways glance.

"The hyacinths were a bit tricky," Jake admitted. "We looked everywhere, having overlooked some right under our nose at my grandfather's greenhouse. They weren't in the conservatory. He has a small conservatory, but we'd missed a walk through the detached greenhouse. I learned something new about him in discovering how much he liked plants and flowers."

"Ah, I see. I do seem to remember a tour of the conservatory once when we had tea with Estelle, your grandmother." Josie smelled the bouquet, breathing in the beautiful scent of the flowers.

"Thank you for the flowers, Hugh," Jill added.

"You're welcome."

"Jillian and I are ready. I'll just be a moment to get my shawl and put these in some water," Josie said, taking both of their bouquets to the kitchen.

When she returned, Hugh had helped Jill into the carriage, and she had a moment alone with Jake as she stepped onto the stoop.

"You look stunning," Jake said in a low voice meant only for her ears as he extended his arm.

"Thank you. You look very handsome this evening, as well," she replied, taking in his dark suit with the teal brocade vest. The suit contrasted well with his blond hair and blue eyes.

"So you knew my grandmother and grandfather well?" he asked as he handed her up into the carriage and she settled into the seat facing her sister and Hugh.

She nodded. "I did. My whole family knew them. We respected and admired them very much."

Jake smiled at this, and for the rest of the drive, they chatted about the weather, the beauty of Cherry Crossing's cherry trees —now in full bloom—and a number of other polite topics. Josie decided against bringing up Blue, politics of any kind, or Jake's campaign for mayor. She thought the topics might ruin the evening. Instead, she and Jill asked if Jake and Hugh had settled in at the mansion, and tidbits about Philadelphia where he and Hugh hailed. She and Jill also shared a few more insights about their farm and the town.

When they arrived in town, they had to wait in line amongst a steady flow of wagons, buggies, carriages, and other conveyances loaded with residents from all around Madison

County. These dropped ladies and children at the front steps of the town hall, a building which also housed the courthouse on the second floor. Gentlemen carrying lanterns helped them find their way inside as it had quickly grown dark. The town hall building, situated across the square from the mayor's mansion, featured an abundance of lanterns and greenery to create a festive ambience. The sound of music streamed outside, and Josie wanted to tap her feet before Jake helped her down from the carriage.

Once inside, they noticed a long row of tables laden with platters of venison, ham, chicken, and roast beef. Piled high with vegetables around the perimeter, the roasted meats caused their mouths to water as they surveyed the delicious foods. More platters of various cheeses and fruits dotted the table, and baskets of breads, rolls, and tarts drew their attention. Casseroles, dishes of vegetables, and desserts aplenty eventually filled in the open spots as ladies brought their best home cooking to share. Pies, tarts, cakes, and other sweets appealed to guests, as well. Jillian stepped aside momentarily to add a huckleberry peach pie to the desserts at the far end as a contribution on behalf of the Hayes sisters, but she returned to their side in time to catch a glimpse of Charlie Martin glaring at Jacqueline and Abel.

To Chad's credit, Josie and her sister noticed he did not glare at Jocelyn or Jake. Charlie may have escorted someone to the dance, but they couldn't tell which lady since a number of them hovered about the Martin boys, all hoping to dance with them. Chad escorted Lydia Ford, the granddaughter of Etta Ford, the owner of Granny's Tea Parlor. Easy to spot, Miss Ford kept her hand firmly planted on Chad's arm as they mingled with their group while guests continued to enter the hall. Miss Ford's presence on his arm came as no surprise to Jocelyn. She had remained Josie's unspoken rival as far back as she could remember, but she paid this no mind. She only wished Chad happiness in life and found herself relieved he had wasted no time in finding someone. It meant her freedom, and she relished the idea Chad no longer harbored ideas about a future with her.

Musicians from all around Madison County and beyond had turned up with an array of fine instruments to delight the crowd. The foursome took in the corner of the hall containing music artists playing violins, banjos, guitars, flutes and trumpets, and drums. Josie recognized the piano from the church. Some men had delivered the instrument to the town hall, and she knew it meant outstanding music would entertain them. Josie returned nods of greeting at some fellow townsfolk passing by, and occasionally someone stopped to mingle for a moment with them.

"I'm impressed with the number of instruments here this evening, considering how far west we are." Hugh commented when the foursome found themselves alone again, marveling at the band assembled there.

Jillian smiled. "We are blessed indeed. People come from the neighboring counties to help us have the very best musicians. Do you play any instruments, Mr. Stanton?"

Hugh chuckled. "Oh no. I'm not musically inclined at all, but Jake plays the piano. I think these four seats along this wall shall be ours for the evening."

"Ah, so does my sister, Jocelyn. She plays beautifully." Jill snapped her fan open and added, "Yes, these seats are fine, don't you think, Josie?"

"Hmm? Yes, these seats are perfect. I'm not that good, really. It pains me to admit it, but I don't practice my piano playing as I should," Josie admitted.

"Do you have a piano at the cabin?" Jake asked.

Josie nodded. "Our father had it shipped here for our mother. She is the one who played so beautifully. I believe there are only four in Madison County. Ours, the one at your mansion which the colonel used to invite my mother and I to play on before we had ours, and the one at the church, and the one at the mission. It's unusual for anyone out west to have one, so we are quite blessed in this area."

"I'm sorry to hear of their passing," Jake added as Hugh nodded. "Your parents, I meant."

"Thank you," Josie replied. "We miss them a great deal."

"Yes, thank you," Jill added. "We do. Some days I'd give anything to hear Ma play again."

"We are also sorry about the loss of your grandparents, and that you weren't able to meet them to my knowledge. They used to talk about you whenever they had news from your mother," Josie explained.

Jake nodded and looked out into the crowd gathering about them as townsfolk continued to stream inside the hall, adding, "Sadly, my mother passed away about a year ago. Consumption. I miss her more than anyone on earth."

He didn't seem to see the people coming inside although he looked in their direction. In fact, he looked a million miles away, Josie thought. They grew silent for a moment out of respect, acknowledging his remarks with empathy in their nods and eyes. Josie wondered if his grandparents had even known of their daughter's passing. First, Estelle had passed away from a severe bout of influenza, and then the colonel from what she suspected could only be a broken heart. He'd seemed so lost without Estelle at his side.

"Ma would want us to dance this evening and celebrate. The Lord above has helped us survive a harsh winter and bestowed us with a successful spring planting," Josie said softly.

"And He has brought my good friend to visit," Jake added, his voice sounding brighter as a smile spread on his face once again. "Another reason to celebrate. We shall have no more talk of sadness on this night." Turning to Josie, he bowed slightly. "May I ask the pleasure of this dance, Miss Hayes?"

She curtsied, lowering her eyes and smiling, excited to dance. "Thank you. I would be delighted."

The opening dance had already played, and a second dance, but now Jake led her onto the dance floor for the third, and she found herself in his capable arms, whirling around and around as the musicians rested while a pianist played a waltz she recognized as "Spring Waltz" by Chopin. The opening notes had always held her captive, and she had worked hard to learn to play the waltz on Ma's piano.

Hugh and Jillian observed from their seats, but they joined in the next dance, as did Jackie and Abel. Josie felt such a thrill to be held so close to Jake, she hardly noticed her sisters after a minute or two, or the fact most eyes in the hall remained riveted on them. Each of her senses heightened as she focused on the gentleman expertly guiding her around the center of the hall among the other couples. She felt as though they glided on air when he whirled her around, and for a while, it seemed like they were the only two people present.

"May I reserve all of your dances for the evening, Miss

Hayes?" Jake asked when he returned her to the seats they'd claimed, spreading their shawls out to mark them.

Josie had nearly forgotten about the dance card she wore on her wrist, given to her at the entrance, but now she looked at it. She reached in her drawstring purse for a pencil and held it out to him with the card to reserve her dances. "Yes, you may." She cared little about what anyone else thought about her dancing the evening away with the handsome and distinguished Mr. Hunter. In fact, looking about the hall, she decided Jake the most handsome of anyone in attendance.

Jacqueline adored dancing with Abel. She stared up at him, taking in everything about his expression, his build, and his aristocratic nose. She liked his manners, the way he looked at her, and how excited he became when he spoke about their expeditions panning for gold at Honey River. He brought her punch and a plate of food when they grew hungry from dancing, but he seemed distracted at times. She could not tell what distracted him or why, but when he disappeared from the hall, she slipped outside in search of him lest they miss the next few dances.

Unable to find him outside in the courtyard and garden where she spotted a couple having a moment alone together, she turned to head back indoors, but Bonnie Stephens, who ran the milliner shop with her husband Craig, stopped to chat with her.

"Miss Hayes, it's so nice to see you. I saw a wonderfully handsome fellow dancing with you. You must tell me all about him. I've not met him yet, but I did see him at Granny's Tea Parlor a few days ago."

Jackie smiled and nodded, happy to speak to someone about her new beau. At least, she considered him among her beaux at this point. She couldn't help but keep a space in her heart for Charlie, but his glares had not impressed her. She hadn't promised herself to him, despite the fact he'd proposed to her no less than three times. "You must be referring to Abel Keller. He is new in town, here with his brother and sister-in-law from Dakota Territory. Have you met Florence?"

Jake returned to their seats with cups of fruit punch for Josie and himself, but he couldn't find her at first. Looking around, he spotted her a few feet away, caught up in a conversation with the banker's wife, Cora Fields. Looking around for Hugh and Jillian, he noticed they appeared deeply involved in a conversation with Reverend Marcus Wells and his wife, Esther. He'd enjoyed the one sermon he'd heard Reverend Wells deliver, but as Hugh had said, he'd found himself distracted by the belligerent beauty who looked so lovely on the pew across the aisle. He promised himself to try and pay better attention the next time the circuit preacher came to town.

His gaze returned to rest on the lovely Jocelyn as he stood by awkwardly, having given up on looking for a place to set their punch glasses down. He could hardly believe she'd agreed to attend the dance with him. So far, the evening had gone well, but he wondered if they could have a future when almost every encounter with her resulted in fire and ice between them. He finally spotted a side table nearby with room enough for their punch glasses and set them down. Still contemplating the complicated dilemma of the stunningly beautiful Josie Hayes as he turned around, a waif in a dark cloak handed him a note.

Opening the folded note written on a scrap of quality paper, it read, *meet me outside in the next few minutes to discuss important information about your grandfather.* He looked up after the girl who'd handed him the note to have a better look at her, but the waif had disappeared into the crowd, and now he couldn't see her anywhere in the dimly lit hall, now full of shadows from the flickering light of candles and lanterns. The fireplace offered the most light but situated on the opposite wall with a crowd of townsfolk between, it lent little help in finding the cloaked figure.

He raked a hand through his hair, wondering what kind of information someone might have about his grandfather. From everything he'd discovered so far, his grandfather's reputation could only be described as nearly impeccable. He couldn't help but wonder if the colonel had made mistakes, too. If so, he might find himself able to connect to the man he'd never known. Thus far, Colonel Harrison Lee Bradshaw seemed larger than life. Letters and medals he'd found in the library proved him a military hero, and as the founder of Honey River Canyon, the townsfolk regarded him a leader who'd become almost legendary. Jake saw him as someone he couldn't live up to, at least not without a generous amount of help from the Lord.

Glancing at the note again, he considered it apprehensively. Did the writer of this note plan to blackmail him for silence with some sort of harmful information about his grandfather?

He supposed at the very least, he should investigate the matter. Since someone else he didn't recognize now pulled Josie deeper into the crowd on his right, and the waif had disappeared into the crowd on his left, and straight ahead, his friend remained firmly ensconced in conversation with the parson, he may as well head outside. He could at least listen and then decide if the information and source deserved any merit.

Chapter Fourteen

Not rendering evil for evil or railing for railing: but contrariwise blessing; knowing that ye are thereunto called, that ye should inherit a blessing.

I Peter 3:9

By the time Josie finished conversing with Cora Fields about Cora's health concerns, latest sewing projects, and hopes for the next missions project as the leader of the Women's Missionary Auxiliary for the local Congregationalist church, she couldn't find any sign of Jake when she returned to their seats against the wall. A glance at Hugh and Jillian standing a few feet away told her they probably hadn't seen Jake either, and they looked happily engaged in pleasant conversation with Reverend and Mrs. Wells.

She looked around the rest of the hall as the musicians continued to play waltzes and many other couples danced, hoping Jake would return in time for the next waltz. It seemed she would have to sit this one out. Too much time had passed since she'd seen Jacqueline with her escort. She studied the gathering of townsfolk again, looking for her middle sister, catching sight of Miss Lydia Ford seated on the other side of the room speaking to Mrs. Twila Thornton, whose husband owned the *Honey River Gazette*, noticing Chad Martin had disappeared from Lydia's side. Perhaps her sister and Abel Keller had stepped outside into the courtyard as couples often did, seeking fresh air to cool down from the dancing, and perhaps a moment of privacy to steal a kiss.

Before Josie could decide whether she should pursue, Ned Wiley burst into the hall through the very doors leading to the courtyard upon which she pondered, hollering, "Is there a doctor in the house? Chad Martin has been shot! We need a doctor!"

His words caused gasps from the ladies, including a gasp escaping from Josie. *Chad Martin, shot? She couldn't fathom it.* The musicians stopped playing at different times causing an eerie sound to fill their ears as the room plunged into a moment of confusion and silence. Some hadn't heard Ned's words, and whispers ran through the hall as people passed along this horrifying development. Seconds later, several gentlemen sprang into action to investigate by following Ned outside, including Charlie and Joshua Martin, Chad's father, closely followed by Sheriff Casey Drummond as he abandoned the preacher's daughter on the dance floor, Elsie Wells.

Chad's mother, Fanny Martin, collapsed near the food

tables where she'd hovered with a few other ladies throughout much of the evening, tending provisions and refilling the punch bowl. The ladies standing nearby attempted to revive her with smelling salts. Chad's sisters, Hope and Joy, rushed to follow Ned and the other men outside, but several mothers stopped the youngest Martin brother, Samuel, from slipping through the doors. Samuel fought them in protest and finally escaped their hold on him.

Honey River Canyon offered many things, but Josie knew no doctor could be found. The town didn't have a doctor yet, and the nearest one involved a harrowing ride to the next county for someone with a gunshot injury. When Rebecca Brooks stepped outside next, Josie exhaled with some relief. Mrs. Brooks often served the community with her medical knowledge and expertise. She had customarily functioned as a midwife, veterinarian, and nurse to the inhabitants of the town for as far back as Josie could remember. Rebecca had tended almost every serious wound or injury in any given emergency until the neighboring doctor in Gallatin County could arrive or be reached.

Josie rose from her seat and crossed the town hall next, unable to sit idly by and wait for news of his condition. Jake still hadn't appeared. She also knew all eyes traveled to her next since everyone suspected she and Chad might marry one day, although Josie now knew they never would. She had meant it when she'd said she would always consider him a good friend, and she had to know what had happened. They'd grown up as neighbor children together, and her mind flooded with fond memories of him. *What if he didn't pull through this? How could someone have shot him? Who would have done such a thing, and why? Dear Lord, please help him.*

Once Josie stepped outside into the courtyard, she followed the commotion to her left which led to the alley between the courthouse and the sheriff's office. A few men held up a lantern in the darkness as folks leaned over Chad, clearing the way for Rebecca to tend him. Josie could hardly see him through the Martin family and men clustered there in the middle of the alley. Tears rose to Josie's eyes as she drew closer. It didn't sound good.

"I'm sorry. He's gone," Rebecca said, rising from where she'd previously knelt. Josie caught a glimpse of Chad's limp body being held in his sisters' arms. The Martin sisters released such desperate wails, it felt like only darkness swallowing them as Josie pushed her way through the crowd to see Chad for herself.

"No, no! Not my brother!" Samuel flung himself over his brother's body, clinging to him as his father tried to pull him away to shield him from the grief-stricken moment.

The men looked somber, most staring at Chad or the ground in sorrow and disbelief, some with stunned looks on their faces. Josie caught sight of Jake in the shadows, hanging back where he'd joined them at some point. Had he walked up the alley from the front of the building?

Chad's father, Joshua, caught sight of Jake, too. Rising with an arm still wrapped around Samuel, he began shouting and pointing at Jake. "You! You weren't inside when this happened. How long have you been wandering around out here?" Chad's father shook a clenched fist, thrusting Samuel into Charlie's arms. "If I find out you did this to become our next mayor and steal Jocelyn Hayes from my son, you'll pay for this Jacob Hunter! I won't rest until I see you hang from the gallows!"

Jake's jaw tightened and his brow went up in surprise at the accusation as Hugh stepped through the crowd to reach his friend's side. Sheriff Drummond stepped between Jake and Joshua Martin. "That's enough, Joshua," the sheriff said in a low voice.

"I didn't have anything to do with this," Jake said, his voice steady and calm. "I was out front, waiting for someone who handed me this note. I didn't set foot in this alley until I heard a commotion."

"Let me see the note," the sheriff said, looking toward Jake.

"You're a liar and a murderer, Hunter! You wanted my son dead so you could be the next mayor and steal Josie. You'll never be half the man your grandfather was, and it was Chad's turn to become our next mayor. You stole that chance from him. You stole everything from him. I know you did, and I'm going to prove it if it's the last thing I do!" Joshua pushed forward against the sheriff and spat in Jake's direction. Jake dodged the vulgar action with a sidestep. Josie's cheeks burned red to hear such accusations and her name mentioned in connection with the ghastly situation.

"My pa is right!" Charlie hollered as he kept Samuel buried against his chest.

"I said enough! Hold your horses, Joshua! You too, Charlie." Sheriff Drummond pushed against Joshua by grabbing his shirt with both hands, thrusting him backwards against Charlie and Samuel. He pointed a finger into Joshua's chest with each of his next words. "Just simmer down, Martin, unless you want to spend the night in a very cold jail cell." The sheriff stepped back and raised his voice to make his next point clear to everyone present. "There will be an investigation, but right now, we don't know who did this. I assure you; I'll do everything in my power to find out who did, but don't go making accusations and assumptions. There's a lotta folks out here wandering around, not just Jake."

Joshua disregarded the sheriff's words as he puffed his chest out, heaving against Drummond toward Jake again. "I'm warning you, Hunter, I ain't finished with you yet! You'll pay for this!"

Sheriff Drummond, Hugh Stanton, and the blacksmith, Abe Cooper—a large burly man—stepped forward in front of Jake to absorb the assault from Joshua Martin's last heavy push against the sheriff in his attempt to hurl words of retribution at Jake. Some other men dragged Joshua away from the sheriff and Jake, insisting Joshua calm down and collect himself. He finally lowered his head and turned toward his son's body with Charlie and Samuel. Rebecca tried to console Hope and Joy as they cried softly at their brother's side. The sheriff clenched his fists, bristling at the whole incident as he stepped out of the fray, pulling Jake and Hugh aside to have a look at the note Jake had mentioned.

Josie could hardly believe her ears and eyes, but she found herself stepping closer to Jake and Hugh to hear the sheriff's discussion. The whole thing seemed like a nightmare. Jake stood tall and still, weathering the storm, as the sheriff read the note. Josie couldn't have been any prouder of Jake for having remained strong and almost entirely silent in the face of such adversity and horrid accusations. Her heart ached for Samuel, Charlie, and all the Martins—and the loss of Chad stunned her.

Some men helped carry Chad to his father's conveyance, and others helped the Martin family assemble to return to their home to grieve and cope with the shock. The sheriff pulled Hugh and Jake closer to the courtyard, and Josie followed but remained some distance away to give them privacy.

Something instinctively told her Jake was innocent, but she had a feeling it would be a fight to clear his name. Swiping at tears running down her cheeks, shaken by Chad's passing and all which had transpired, she only wanted to go home, and she still hadn't found Jackie.

Hugh stepped up beside them and noticed her trembling hand. She hadn't realized how much it was shaking until then. "Come with me, Miss Hayes. Let's find your sister and wait in the carriage for Jake while he finishes speaking to the sheriff. Ah, here is Jillian now with your shawl and other belongings. Let's head toward the carriage."

Chapter Fifteen

A hypocrite with his mouth destroyeth his neighbor: but
through knowledge shall the just be delivered.

Proverbs 11:9

Hugh led Jillian and Jocelyn to the carriage where the driver
waited for them, each sister clinging to the other. As soon as
they'd settled inside, Josie conferred with Jill, wondering what
had become of Jackie. "I haven't seen her for a long while," she
said, drawing her shawl close about her shoulders.

Jill bit her lower lip. "We shan't worry. I am convinced
Abel's absence means he has driven her home to shield her from
these spectacularly horrid events. Someone came inside the hall
and told us Chad is gone. It's so hard to believe he's gone, just
like that, in an instant..." Her voice faded away.

Josie nodded, swiping more tears away. "It's all been such a shock. I hope you are right about Abel taking Jackie home." Josie didn't feel right, and she could hardly process her thoughts. Shuddering, she tried to sink into the velvet cushions and wait patiently for Jake. She needed a hot cup of tea and her bed.

"You look so pale, Josie. I'm worried about you." Jill stared at her from beside Hugh as he handed out the lap blankets. "You and Chad have always been close friends."

Josie nodded again, biting her lower lip. "It's going to take time to accept the fact he's gone."

Hugh sighed. "I don't even know what to say to offer any words of comfort to you ladies. I didn't know Chad Martin, but I'm very sorry for your loss. I'm sure he was a fine and respected fellow in the community. His father's actions come from a heart of grief and enormous loss. I hope this can all get sorted out and Jake's name cleared."

Josie nodded. "Thank you, Mr. Stanton. I hope so, too."

"What did Chad's father do?" Jill inquired. "I didn't see it, but I heard he was shouting at Jake. He doesn't really believe Jake had anything to do with this, does he?"

Hugh nodded. "Unfortunately, yes, he does. He made quite a scene outside the courthouse." They sank into silence, and Josie tried to push the words Joshua Martin had spoken from her mind.

Hugh looked up and shifted in his seat. "Here comes Jake now. Looks like he's done speaking to the sheriff so we can all go home." He drew in a breath of relief and exhaled, concern written in his furrowed brows.

Jake climbed into the carriage and tapped his cane for the driver. "To Cherry Crossing, Ollie, and then home."

Ollie nodded and pulled out into traffic with a long line of other conveyances, all making their way to their homes, everyone saddened by what had transpired. Some townsfolk walked with their heads down, and Jake's party drove along in silence in similar fashion until they reached the countryside where no other wagons rumbled along near them.

Jake finally broke the silence first. "Disastrous, despicable, and dreadful turn of events. Are you all right, Miss Hayes? Of course you are not, but I find myself at a loss for the right sort of words in this moment."

She nodded as he took her gloved hand in his. "I'm not all right, but I will eventually be, and thank you for asking. I shudder to think of how Joshua treated you. It was uncalled for."

"People sometimes say and do awful things in their grief. I'm terribly sorry about what has happened to your friend. I understand you are neighbors to the Martin cattle ranch, and I've heard the brothers have helped Cherry Crossing a great deal over the years," Jake said, causing her to wonder how he knew this. Perhaps his employed servants had filled him in, or someone in town.

Josie nodded. "Yes, we grew up together, playing as children in the creeks, riding ponies, attending school together back when we only had the church building for a school. We walked to town together on most school days. It's hard to believe this has happened. I can't imagine who would have done such a thing. Everyone liked Chad." His only flaw had been his ego, but as the son of the most successful cattle farmer in the region,

111

she supposed it understandable and had always tried to over-look it.

Jake squeezed her hand and gave her an understanding and compassionate look. Then he turned toward his friend from Philadelphia. "It sounds a lot like how Hugh and I were over the years. Neighbors, friends, school chums, university pals..." Then he added, "Hugh, thank you for helping the ladies while I spoke to the sheriff."

"Of course. Are we going to need an attorney?" Hugh asked.

"Possibly, but I hope not. When I showed the sheriff this note given to me by some waif-like girl I've never seen before, he and I both conclude someone tried to set me up to make it look like I shot Chad."

Jill gasped as Jake reached inside his morning coat and with-drew the note. He handed it to Hugh, who read it by holding it near the carriage light, and then Hugh handed it to Josie.

"This is disturbing indeed. Did you find anyone outside?" Josie asked after reading it. "I don't recognize this handwriting at all." She passed the note to Jill.

"No, I never did find anyone outside. But I have a hunch if we can find the girl in the cloak who gave it to me, we can discover who asked her to deliver it. Then I think we'll be closer to knowing who did this." Jake sounded hopeful, but as they continued the discussion, they realized none among them had seen the girl in the cloak. Perhaps someone else had, but for now, they had no idea about her identity.

For the remainder of the ride, Jill and Josie tried to guess the identity of the waif by asking Jake questions, but his vague answers left them with few clues.

Chapter Sixteen

What time I am afraid, I will trust in thee.

Psalm 56:3

Finding Jacqueline at home gave Josie and her younger sister a great deal of relief when Jake had finished escorting them to the door of the cabin. She would have invited him inside, but she knew he and Hugh faced the drive back to town, and her frayed nerves only longed for a cup of hot tea and the comfort of her bed. Jackie had already fallen asleep, so she didn't bother to question her after peeking inside her bedroom. She closed the door and went directly to her room to change into something more comfortable, thankful when Jillian brought them both a cup of steaming bergamot tea. The flavor calmed and soothed her, and before long, she fell into a deep sleep from the emotionally charged, exhausting evening.

On Sunday, she and her sisters stayed home from church and burrowed under the covers, resting for most of the day. She didn't dare go into town to withstand the whispers and stares of suspicion cast upon Jake Hunter, not to mention the fact Joshua Martin had mentioned her name in connection to his motive. The rumors as people repeated Joshua's words would circulate all over town in the next day or two, and she couldn't bear to face any of it yet. She had her own grief to contend with over the loss of her friend and the sorrow she knew his family would have to cope with for years to come. Remembering when her parents had passed, she knew the pain and sorrow of loss deeply. She also knew healing from the loss would take more time than anyone bargained.

When she did rise, Josie dressed quickly and made a pot of tea and a plate of bland scrambled eggs and toast. She stepped outside to retrieve the Sunday morning newspaper on the stoop. A local farm boy delivered their subscription. Opening it to read the headline of the *Honey River Gazette* while she ate breakfast broke her heart for Jake and Chad. The headline read, "Mayor's Grandson Accused of Murder." The story mentioned every detail except the fact Jake had been lured outside with a note given to him by an unknown girl. Perhaps leaving the detail out would help Jake in the long run. If the waif realized he needed to find her, she might run away. Still, to see his name smeared in the newspaper broke her heart as much as it did to read about the loss of her friend. Now the accusation would spread considerably faster, and the article had the nerve to mention her name in connection to Jake's motive again.

Josie stepped to the cookstove and reached for a thick cloth. She folded the cloth to make it thicker and then wrapped it around the burner handle. She lifted the handle to remove the burner over the fire she'd made inside. Then she fed the fire the newspaper, despising the words contained therein.

With tears in her eyes, she finished her breakfast, leaving plenty of scrambled eggs in the frying pan on the cookstove for her sisters to eat at their leisure. Then she headed outside to tend to the stock. After this, she returned to her room and sat on her bed reading the Psalms, communing with the Lord for strength, praying for truth and justice to prevail. She believed with all her heart in Jake's innocence but proving it with little or no evidence of who had murdered Chad remained entirely another matter. She could hear her sisters move about in the cabin from time to time, but they stayed to themselves to process their grief, too.

The bleakness of the situation alarmed her, and her eyes filled to the brim with tears time and again as she thought about it. Would her hopes of finding true love and a blissful future with Jake Hunter be dashed upon the rocks of false accusations before they could even bloom? The weight of his predicament crushed her soul, and to make matters worse, it seemed she had to sit idly by as her hopes and dreams faded while the sheriff conducted his investigation. It hardly seemed fair.

Monday morning arrived after Josie had shed too many tears to count. Her soul felt numb, but she knew she had to go forward trusting God. The Holy Spirit had comforted her, leading her to a verse she'd relied upon for comfort in the past when she had needed the Lord's protection, Isaiah 54:17. *No weapon formed against thee shall prosper; and every tongue that shall rise against thee in judgment thou shalt condemn. This is the heritage of the servants of the Lord, and their righteousness is of me, saith the Lord.*

Josie found herself reciting the verse multiple times as she dressed, ate breakfast with her sisters, finished her morning chores, and headed to the barn to saddle Mrs. Velvet. She'd head to the mission, hoping they wouldn't take the news about the dastardly murder too hard. Participating in future community dances looked more unlikely than ever for the mission once they heard the news, if they hadn't already.

Before she could finish saddling Mrs. Velvet, a knock on the barn doors disrupted her thoughts. "May I come in, Josie?" She thought she'd heard a buggy drive up close to the cabin.

Josie recognized the voice, but it sounded very much out of place. "Mother Marta! Yes, of course, come in. I was just saddling Mrs. Velvet to head to the mission. What brings you to Cherry Crossing?"

"I'm sorry to bother you, Josie, but I knew you'd want to know right away. Star and her sister, Robin, have disappeared. One of your sisters said you'd be in the barn, so here I am, pleading for your help."

Josie gulped, her brows furrowing as she stood still to consider the news. "Disappeared?"

Marta nodded. "Yes, they disappeared sometime Saturday night or early Sunday morning, and we sent a search party out on Sunday immediately after the chapel service, but they haven't found them yet. Bishop Thomas and Padre Cornelius are continuing the search today, but they went toward the east. I wanted you to know because the girls might find their way here. They said their prayers with the other students as usual on

Saturday night before bed, but when they didn't come down-stairs for breakfast or chapel, we realized they were missing."

Josie nodded. "It's possible they may have tried to come to Cherry Crossing, I suppose. What if they changed their minds along the way? Where else might they have gone?"

"I don't know. We've looked everywhere, in town, knocking on doors in the countryside around the mission, but we don't really know. In fact, we were hoping you might have some ideas," the nun confessed.

Josie bit her lower lip as she considered the matter. "The mountains. Robin loves the mountains. I think she'd convince her big sister to take her there. She's always looking at them, studying them with a longing in her eyes."

Marta tilted her head to one side. "The mountains? Any idea which one?"

"They're so young. I don't think they'd make it as far as Silver Mountain and Cherry Crossing easily. In fact, I'd be surprised if they made it much farther than Canyon Lake and Gold Mountain," Josie remarked with a pensive tone.

"Bishop Thomas and Padre Cornelius searched all around Canyon Lake and even as far north as along Honey Creek yesterday. They didn't find them in those areas," Marta explained, "but it doesn't mean they weren't a little farther along near the mountains. I don't think they would go too far... unless someone took them in a wagon or something. You may very well be right that they are somewhere up on one of these mountains." Mother Marta stepped near the barn doors to look at the mountains in the distance over-looking the valley. Today, their tops looked purple where the misty morning clouds swirled around them, and the rest of the mountains shared various shades of green, gray, and brown.

Josie turned back to finish saddling Mrs. Velvet and tightened the belt beneath the mare's girth. "Let's hope they haven't gone for a ride with any strangers. My guess is Gold Mountain then. It's closest to the mission. I'll ride directly there and start looking. I'm glad you came to tell me. I won't stop looking until I find them."

"Thank you, Josie, but please take some supplies, and do be careful going up the mountain. I'll try to send someone to help you as soon as possible." Marta stepped forward to pat the mare. "She's beautiful, by the way. I can see why you're hoping to find the perfect stallion now that I've met her."

"Thank you," Josie replied, pausing to admire the mare with the nun. "I'm sure you've heard about Chad."

Mother Marta nodded. "Yes. I'm very sorry to hear the news. I read all about it in the *Honey River Gazette*. I know you knew him well. I figured your heart would be in great distress of soul."

Josie nodded. "Yesterday was very hard. They are blaming Jake, but I believe he is innocent."

"Jake would never do such a thing. I know I've only just met him the one time, but he's much too nice a fellow to get mixed up into something like this. I'm sure it was a terribly hard day for you. I'm praying." The nun gave her a warm hug. "Godspeed."

"Godspeed," she agreed, watching Mother Marta leave the barn.

With no time to lose, Jocelyn didn't waste much time observing the Mother Superior as she climbed into her buggy and snapped the reins gently, driving away toward the mission with her black habit blowing softly in the breeze. First, she needed to pray, and then pack some food and extra water, and change into an old calico dress and walking boots suitable for mountain climbing. *Dear Lord, please grant me success in my mission to find Robin and Star, and keep them safe until You lead me to them. Thank you in advance. Amen.*

Chapter Seventeen

Consider it pure joy, my brothers and sisters, whenever you face
trials of many kinds, because you know that the testing of your
faith produces perseverance. Let perseverance finish its work so
that you may be mature and complete, not lacking anything.

James 1:2-4, NIV

Josie eyed Gold Mountain from astride Mrs. Velvet. Tall and
foreboding, she refused to let the view from the ground deter
her. She would ride the mare as far as they could climb together,
and then tie the horse to a tree if she had to keep going on foot
when it became too steep. Before starting her journey, she
cupped her hands around her mouth and called out, "Robin!
Star! Girls?" Only the echo of her own words replied, but she
prayed the Lord would lead her to them.

She considered the two trails leading to the top and chose the one on her left, looking for any sign of travelers. She looked for footprints along the trail but didn't see any. She knew of a mountain man who lived up on Silver Mountain, but he hardly ever came down except a few times each year for supplies. As they climbed up the side of Gold Mountain, Josie spotted a cluster of huckleberry shrubs in the foliage causing her to remember the first time she'd seen them as a child, new to Wyoming Territory, exploring Silver Mountain. They wouldn't produce fruit until later in the summer, but she could almost taste them. The bluish-purple berries tasted a little sweet and reminded her of the same texture as eating a grape.

Thinking about the berries caused her to consider the hunger and thirst facing Robin and Star by this time, and she wondered if they'd taken any provisions along with them. Jillian had packed some egg salad sandwiches, apples, and other items into her saddle bag, and she had two canteens of water, plus a bedroll in case a warm blanket might come in handy. When Mrs. Velvet had carried her a few more yards, she stopped the horse and called out again for the girls, listening for any sign of response. Nothing. Only her own echo again. They continued the climb, plodding along slowly so the mare wouldn't lose her footing in the rocky places, and taking care to stay on the trail.

"Mother Marta! How nice to see you again. Have you met my friend, Hugh Stanton, from Philadelphia?" Jake greeted the nun Brent Tolliver ushered into the library, surprised she would take time to visit with the rigorous mission work he guessed she had on her plate. He'd, of course, told Tolliver to show her in, knowing a good reason for her call lurked somewhere.

Hugh stepped forward to shake her hand and bow slightly. "A pleasure to meet you, ma'am."

"And you," the nun replied, nodding in his direction after shaking his hand.

"Please, make yourself comfortable. Would you like any tea?" Jake asked, indicating the comfortable leather chairs drawn up to the fireplace in a cozy grouping.

"No, I won't require tea. I'm just passing by on my way back to the mission, and I thought you might like to know two of our orphan girls disappeared on Sunday."

Jake's brows furrowed. "Oh, this is distressing news, indeed. How old are the girls?"

"Ten and twelve. Their names are Robin and Star. Two little Indian girls. They are darlings and have never given us the slightest bit of trouble, but they are very fond of one of our part-time teachers, a Miss Jocelyn Hayes, whom I believe you may know." Mother Marta paused. "She teaches our students French and assists us with a great many other duties around the mission. In passing, she may have mentioned you and Hugh would escort her and one of her sisters to the spring dance."

"Correct," Jake said, wondering where the nun would take the conversation. He hadn't seen the orphans, and didn't know if he could help, but it sounded urgent. He also had to clear his name, and to do so, he had to find the waif-like character who'd handed him the note. Over the next few days, he planned to ride all over town and then scour the countryside, knocking on every door if required. In fact, if she'd arrived much later, Mother Marta would likely have missed them both. They'd just finished breakfast, and Hugh planned to ride around searching with him, but how could he in good conscience turn his back on the plight of two helpless children, and orphans no less?

The nun standing before them in the library continued. "I've just come from Cherry Crossing in case the girls decided to attempt to visit Miss Hayes, and now Josie is on her way up Gold Mountain to look for them. A search party sent out yesterday from our mission failed to find the girls. I told Josie I would try to send more help her way." The nun finished explaining the situation, and as soon as Jake heard Josie's name, he reached for his suit jacket. Knowing Josie had gone in search of the girls by herself clinched his decision. Clearly, he must lay aside his plans to assist Miss Hayes in finding the orphan girls. Returning honor to his grandfather and his name would have to wait.

"Did you say Josie went up Gold Mountain in search of the girls?" Jake attempted to straighten his tie and the lapels of his suit coat, wondering which of the mountains behind the mansion bore the name. They all looked a little golden to him at sunset and sunrise. Arthur could tell him the exact location of this mountain.

The nun nodded. "Yes, that's the one she'll begin her search upon. I think she planned to ride the black mare. She won't rest until she finds them. She's quite determined, you know, and very attached to Robin and Star."

Jake acknowledged her remarks with raised brows, an emphatic and knowing nod, and a peculiar smile while a coughing fit escaped Hugh. He'd heard all about Josie and could barely contain his amusement with the nun's remarks. Jake tried to temper his reply. "Yes, we've experienced the determination of Miss Hayes." In truth, he couldn't measure the respect he'd gained for her in the short time since he'd arrived. He certainly could not argue the fact she had more gumption and determination than any woman he'd ever known, except perhaps his own mother.

"She gave him quite the lecture about buying his stallion when my friend Jake here, unknowingly purchased it, as I understand." Hugh clapped him on the back good-naturedly. "Better you to aggravate your belligerent beauty than me, my friend."

Mother Marta failed in her attempt to hide her smile. "I may have heard a little something about the matter, but now I understand a little more."

Jake took the suit coat off after putting it on. "On second thought, I think we should change into something more suitable for a mountain expedition and have Maddie pack us a lunch. We'll need some canteens with plenty of water."

"Thank you, Jacob Hunter. I knew I could count on you and Mr. Stanton. I'd best return to the children before the mission falls down in my absence." Mother Marta shook hands with them again, and turned to go, adding over her shoulder, "I'll be praying for you all. At this point, you are our only hope, and may the Lord reward you richly, and lead your efforts."

Jake hurried to walk the nun out into the hall. "Thank you, Mother Marta. We'll do everything we can. I'm sure we'll find them. They couldn't have gone very far."

"Your words mean a great deal to us at a time like this. I shall tell Padre Cornelius when he returns from his searching today. He will be most thankful for your endeavors." A servant held the door open for her as she lifted her black habit a little and stepped outside, and Jake marveled as he watched her leave. For a woman well in her fifties he guessed, she still had a sprightly bounce in her step, an abundance of energy, a Holy Spirit glow, and apparent good health. For a moment, he wondered if reading the Bible, immersing herself in prayer, or holiness contained the secret to her glow, but he had a feeling all three contributed to her appeal and wellbeing. As a preacher, he could only hope his efforts followed in her footsteps and had the same results. Every sin seemed to have set him back and cost him dearly, but murder wasn't one of them. Jake returned to the library, raking a hand through his blond hair, thinking, for the first time in his life, he must contend with thoughts of such an exclusion. Had coming to Montana Territory been a huge mistake? Things seemed truly wild out here where some men had no respect for civility, the sanctity of human life, and the law. Now he understood why they called it the Wild West, and today he felt trapped in it.

When Hugh heard the front doors close out in the hall, he put his hands in his pockets and watched Jake as he paced momentarily inside the library while gathering his thoughts. "You saw the black habit the nun is wearing. Now was the cape on the waif-creature black, or was it blue?"

Jake stopped pacing and turning to look at him in surprise because they had returned to this topic at this moment, shrugged. "I don't know. I've been thinking on it since you first asked me at breakfast. Maybe it was black. It was too dark to get a good look. It didn't have the white thing around her head which nuns wear. She wore a hood, and I think it was lined with the same dark fabric, but I need to ponder it some more. What kind of sandwiches do you want and how many? We could be on the mountain a long time."

"Better yet, maybe I should look for the waif, and you help Josie," Hugh suggested. "I'd say four or five sandwiches ought to be sufficient."

"You might have a good plan there." Jake wondered what could go wrong next as they rounded the corner to the kitchen, running directly into the plump housekeeper. "Maddie, dear ... if I could have a word."

Maddie put her hands on her hips and smirked. "You sound just like your grandfather when he wanted something. Out with it. What is it you want?" She looked from Jake to Hugh and back again as if they were guilty of high treason.

"About our lunch, Mrs. Penworth, could you prepare about eight ... no, ten ... maybe twelve chicken salad sandwiches, some of those delicious peaches, and plenty of the banana bread with the walnuts in it? Oh, and some canteens of water, too. We're going on a long hike. Well, I'm going on a long hike up a mountain in search of some orphans who disappeared, and Hugh is searching for... well never mind that part. In any case, we'll need the lunches packed, half in each of two saddle bags, easy to carry on horseback. Maybe some carrots in case the horses need a little prodding. And we're leaving shortly, so we need it pronto. I read the word in a Wild West story in a newspaper. It is a word out here, right? Maybe throw in some extra food in case I'm stuck overnight."

Maddie laughed. "Yes indeed, Master Hunter, but slow down. I can barely keep up with you. Pronto means on the double, or quick. I'll see what I can have our cooks rustle up for you, sir. Check back with the kitchen in five or ten minutes. Does this mean you'll not be home for dinner?"

"I'm not sure. I have a feeling it could be a long day," Jake said. "I have no idea."

"I'll never tire of hearing them call you Master Hunter." Hugh snickered. "Do you pay them extra for the honor?"

Jake rolled his eyes at Hugh, but he smiled good-naturedly. Ignoring him, he turned his attention back to Maddie when she asked, "What's this about missing orphans? From the mission?"

Jake nodded. "Robin and Star have gone missing."

"Oh no! 'Tis wretched to think of some precious orphans disappearing. I wondered why Tolliver said the Mother Superior was here. We'll fix your lunches up at once. If anyone can find them, sir, you can. You have your grandfather's blood running through your veins, and he would have gone in search of them, too. He was a war hero, you know. I can't get over the similarities between you, sir." Maddie turned toward the kitchen staff and hollered for the scullery maid causing Jake to nearly jump out of his skin. "Mar-jor-eeeee!"

Jake led them away from the kitchen as the kitchen maid scurried to Maddie's side. "Hugh, you won't need to change since you'll be riding through town and countryside. You are dressed comfortably to do so, are you not?"

Hugh nodded, straightening his tie. "I am fine in my suit. I can't very well show up on doorsteps asking questions, not looking my best. I'll ask Tolliver to ready two horses. If I return before you, I'll content myself to read a book or find something amusing to pass the time after dinner. Arthur said he might be up for another game of chess, and I am determined to beat him this time."

"Very good. Arthur plays a mean game of chess. I'll change into some old work clothes and meet you in the stable in a few." Jake headed down the hall toward the staircase. He couldn't help but take some degree of comfort in the fact Maddie believed in him and saw something of the grandfather he'd never met inside him. Taking the steps two at a time, he had little time to lose. Ever since he'd read the newspaper article on Sunday, more doubts filled his mind and heart, but at least Maddie still believed in him.

He couldn't say for sure how Josie felt about him after all of this, but if one person remained in Honey River Canyon who still believed in him, then perhaps he shouldn't sell out to the gold prospector and cut his ties. Lately, the offer sounded better than ever, but if he could clear his name, maybe he could make a go of it out here in the wilds of Montana.

First, he had to catch up to Josie, find the orphans, and then the waif. He'd missed seeing the beautiful Miss Hayes in church yesterday, and the circuit preacher hadn't delivered a sermon. Someone else had on his behalf, but the message had barely sustained him because he hadn't found it easy to concentrate while attempting to ignore the stares from curious onlookers. They'd obviously read the newspaper or attended the dance and heard the gossip. He also hadn't realized Honey River Canyon only had a circuit preacher until Hugh had informed him on Sunday at the afternoon meal of his and Jillian's extensive conversation with the minister and his wife at the dance. This information preoccupied a corner of his mind on top of every-thing else, given his background. No, he couldn't possibly consider stepping up to shepherd a church, owning and over-seeing the trading post and the mansion he'd inherited from his grandfather, and taking on the role of mayor—could he? As he finished changing into a pair of overalls and an old shirt he'd often worn around his father's farm, he laughed out loud at himself. First, he had to clear his name, and he couldn't begin to do it without the Lord's help.

Prayer! Of course, he should start there, as he had on Sunday morning in church before he'd become so distracted with the stares from townsfolk. *Lord, I could really use your help. Please bless Hugh's efforts today, and help me find the orphans, and protect Josie. And please get me out of this mess.*

Chapter Eighteen

When my glory passes by, I will put you in a cleft in the rock
and cover you with my hand until I have passed by.

Exodus 33:22, NIV

"Josie! Robin! Star!" Jake cupped his hands over his mouth and
hollered out at the beginning of the trail he'd chosen. He'd
picked the one on the left, thinking the children might have
selected the one closest to the mission. No reply except for his
own echo. He urged the horse forward, and they began to
climb, his eyes scanning everything.

Arthur had helped to set him straight, pointing out which
mountain he needed to ride toward, and the direction of the
mission. He'd passed it before when riding Tornado, and now
the black stallion would prove his worth climbing it. He only

hoped Miss Hayes wouldn't lecture him at once upon seeing the stallion. He knew she had her heart set on him selling him to her, but he still wrestled with the idea since he'd grown fond of the horse. Tornado had a good temperament, and he obeyed every command without delay. A steep climb ahead, he prayed for Godspeed and continued, hoping to catch up to Josie if he didn't take any breaks for a while.

After two hours of riding, pausing every twenty to thirty minutes to call out for the girls, Josie began to experience weariness as the sun beat down on her and Mrs. Velvet. "Just a little further, Mrs. Velvet, and there's a stream up ahead." She patted the mare to encourage her and pulled her bonnet on more securely to shade her eyes from the bright sunshine, cherishing the shady areas when they encountered wooded areas thick with fir, pine, and spruce trees.

Reaching the stream, Josie chose a sunny spot and dismounted, shivering because of the cooler temperature as she climbed closer to the snowy peaks. She led her horse to drink from the brook. Wrapping herself in the shawl she'd brought, she drank some fresh water from the canteen and sat down on a grassy patch to eat a sandwich after tying the mare to a tree, convinced she had to be close to the girls. She didn't think they'd have climbed much higher without facing extreme exhaustion for their ages. The snow-capped peaks at the top caused her to shiver as she considered the cold night they may have faced. She ate the sandwich in silence, listening for any sounds of life. Some birds caught her attention as they sang out to each other, and a squirrel scampering away made her turn her head. Her eyes widened, catching sight of a blue ribbon tangled in a shrub some yards away, uncannily like the one she'd given Robin to give to Star. She dropped the sandwich onto the brown paper her sister had wrapped it in, rising with her mouth open. Had the Lord sent the squirrel to gain her attention? *Thank you, Lord.*

She drew closer to the shrub and touched the ribbon, slowly untangling it from the shrub. She called out, "Robin! Star! Are you there? Girls?"

Josie waited, listening with all her might. Muffled, desperate voices replied. Voices she recognized but couldn't see anywhere. They sounded close, but far away all at the same time, coming from her left, but farther ahead a little. "Miss Hayes! Miss Hayes! We're here! We're down here!"

"Girls! I'm here! Keep talking! I can't see you!" she called back, following their voices when she heard them call out, "Help us! Please help us!"

Josie continued to follow the voices up the mountain, but the closer she drew to them, the worse she felt as it led her too close to a rocky edge where the trees had thinned out. She'd had to leave the trail, as well. "Keep talking, girls!"

"We're down here, on the side of the mountain, Miss Hayes!" Star's voice. This time, the response sounded so close she realized she'd just passed them, but she still couldn't see them anywhere she looked. She had a knot in the pit of her stomach, realizing they must be somewhere on the side of the mountain, stuck in a dangerous spot.

"Keep talking to me, Star. Are you all right? Is Robin all right?" she asked, drawing closer to the edge of the mountain.

She didn't have to holler as much to be heard and figured she must be right above them. Dropping to the ground, she crawled on her hands and knees to the edge, not terribly fond of heights.

"We're scared, but we're okay," Star replied.

Josie reached the edge, and now she inched forward on her belly until she could peer over the edge, praying she wouldn't feel sick when she looked down. She took in the sight as her stomach lurched at the view so far below them. Yet, the Lord had kept them, huddled together, safe and sound in a cleft of rock jutting out on the side of a very steep place on Gold Mountain.

"Oh, girls! I've found you at last..." she breathed, trying to sound calm. The view below the cleft where they clung to each other, burrowed into the side of the mountain, made Josie sick to her stomach. She blinked, forcing herself to only look at the girls as they turned tear-stained cheeks with smiles of relief toward her.

"Hang on girls. I'm going to find a way to get you out of there." Josie wondered how they had fallen there. They had to have dropped a good four or five feet.

"Thank God, you found us! We pr-prayed, M-Miss Hayes. We prayed really hard," Robin said, her voice quivering.

"How did you get down there?" she asked.

"We saw a black bear, and he saw us, and he growled. Then he chased after us, so we ran, and we shimmied down here where he couldn't find us. He finally gave up waiting for us. I think he became distracted, forgot about us, and wandered away. But then we were stuck and couldn't get back up to the top again," Star explained.

"You were very smart to hide from the bear, and the Lord

protected you, and He answered your prayers and led me to you. Hang on girls. I have to go back to my horse and figure out a way to pull you up," Josie said. "Stay very still. Don't move. I'll be right back, okay?"

"Yes, ma'am. Please hurry," Robin said. Star nodded.

Their eyes appeared hauntingly desperate, and Josie knew they were terrified, but hopeful. "I'm going to get you out of this. Just keep praying and I will be right back."

Josie backed away from the edge, terror striking her own heart. The girls remained in a tremendously precarious situation. Amazed, she realized the Lord had protected them in the cleft. She needed rope and strength, but it hadn't occurred to her to bring any rope. *Lord, help me, please.*

When she had crawled and turned away from the edge a safe enough distance to stand without feeling too dizzy, Josie stood, trying to keep her nerves calm. She returned to the horse, thinking about what she had to use to rescue the girls. She heard a twig snap, diverting her attention, and a voice calling her name—a man's voice. *Jake!*

She looked toward the trail leading down the mountain, and around the bend, Jake emerged from the thick foliage, riding on Blue. "Jake! I can't tell you how happy I am to see you." Her voice broke into a wide smile. "Mother Marta said she'd send help, but I was expecting Padre Cornelius or Bishop Thomas." The idea the nun may have played a game of matchmaking crossed her mind, but she had no time to waste pondering it. They had to rescue Robin and Star.

When he reached her, Jake dismounted. "Are you all right? You look white as a ghost."

She nodded. "I'm not okay, but I will be. Please tell me you have some rope with you."

He took her hands in his, still holding the reins to Blue. "I've got plenty of rope, a knife, food, some canvas, two bedrolls, and water. Arthur and Maddie equipped me. You're trembling."

"I found the girls," she explained. "It's not good. They're four or five feet down the side of the mountain on a ledge. It's like a cleft in the rock. It's about yay wide." She motioned with her hands to approximate the narrow width. "About three or four feet at most. The drop below them is... I can't... I can't even speak of it." She squeezed her eyes shut, dizzy from remembering it.

"All right, take it easy. We're going to get them up from there safe and sound. Okay?"

She nodded, burying her head in his chest as he pulled her close and wrapped his arms around her shoulders. She gathered her composure, drawing strength from his presence and confidence, utterly thankful Mother Marta had thought to send him.

He turned to Blue, removing a length of rope from his saddle bag. "Take me to them."

She led him toward the girls, thankful he didn't ask how they'd gotten into this predicament. He got right down to business, ready to proceed with the rescue. "I can't look down again. I just can't. I'll be sick," she whispered so the girls wouldn't hear the fear in her voice as they approached.

"It's all right. You won't have to," he promised, tying a slip-knot in the length of rope as they walked. "Just point me to the area. I'll do the rest, stay close behind me, and do exactly as I ask if needed."

"Okay. I can do that," she said, lowering her voice since they drew close to the cleft over the side of the mountain. "Watch your step here. It's rocky," she cautioned. Then she called out gently to the girls. "Jake Hunter is here to help, girls. Do exactly as he says, and we can all go home shortly."

"Yes, M-m-miss Hayes," Star returned with her shaky voice. "We're here."

Jake did the same thing she'd done previously, crawling on all fours toward the edge, and then dropping to his belly to inch forward until he could look over it and down at the orphans. "Hello girls."

Star must have looked up at him, Josie figured with a relieved smile. "Hello, Mr. Jake. We're very glad to see you." Josie shuddered to think how frightened Robin must be since she'd hardly spoken.

Josie observed Jake take in the situation and then speak calmly. "I'm going to lower some rope, and then you must slip it around your waist, grab on to it with both hands firmly, and I'll pull you up, one at a time. Understand?"

"Yes, Mr. Jake," Star said. Taking charge, they heard her say, "Robin, you go first."

Jake dropped the rope down. "Yep, just like that. Slip it over your head and move it down around your waist. Star, you're brilliant. You know exactly what to do. Good job, Robin. Ready?"

Josie heard Robin's smaller voice say, "I'm ready."

Jake wasted no time. "One, two, and three." In seconds, he pulled Robin up and over the steep mountain edge. Robin burst into giggles and tears at the same time, throwing her arms around his neck. "Thank you, thank you, Mister Jake." Then she closed her eyes, clasped her hands together, and bowed her head. "Thank you, Lord Jesus." Next, she slipped the rope off and stood, brushing herself off before flinging herself into Josie's arms. "Thank you, Miss Hayes! Now let's get my sister, please." She understood the severity of the situation. Her gaze turned to Jake for Star's safety, and she quieted down quickly, watching Jake as he checked the rope to be sure of the slip knot.

Then he repeated the same steps, and within seconds, he hoisted Star up and over the edge.

"Thank you, Lord Jesus for sending Mister Jake and Miss Josie to our rescue." Star made the sign of the cross over herself. Then she flung herself into Jake's arms as he backed away from the edge, pulling them to a more secure spot. Star buried her head in his arms, bursting into sobs. A minute later, she looked over at Josie and her sister, a wide smile and thankful, relieved expression appearing as tears streamed down her face.

Chapter Nineteen

Howbeit, Jesus suffered him not, but saith unto him, go home to thy friends, and tell them how great things the Lord hath done for thee, and hath had compassion on thee.

Mark 5:19

Josie and Jake led the girls over to the stream and let them wipe their tears away, washing their hands and faces in the stream. Josie wrapped them both in a blanket, worried about how cold their bodies seemed after the number of hours they'd spent on a cold rock ledge. She sat them down and offered water from the canteen. Thirsty, they drank again and again while Josie laid out sandwiches. Jake stepped over to his saddle bag and brought more delicious food to the picnic. As they all ate to their hearts' content, Josie relayed the story about how they'd ended up in their predicament, telling him about the black bear. The girls jumped into telling the story, too. Jake commended the girls for their bravery, and before long, the girls began to grow sleepy.

"As much as we want to go home to the mission, we are so tired, Miss Hayes. I don't know if we can make the trip down this mountain yet," Star admitted, her eyelids drooping from heaviness. "We only ran away because we wanted to go to the dance, and to sit by you, and to learn how to dance."

Robin nodded to everything Star had said, but she looked even sleepier.

"I know girls, and we're working on trying to change the policy. Perhaps one day soon, you will be able to go to all the community dances. Did you sleep at all?" Josie asked.

Robin and her sister shook their heads no, but Robin answered for them. "We were too afraid we'd roll off the ledge in our sleep. Do you know how many times I've fallen out of bed in the middle of the night?"

They laughed together about Robin's answer. Jake said, "I'm guessing you sleep in bunk beds at the mission." The girls nodded, and he added, "I think it was wise of you not to fall asleep on the rock ledge."

Robin closed her eyes, shivering despite the sunshine. "If we could just rest here a little while, then we'll be ready."

Josie and Jake nodded and agreed to wait, watching the girls fall asleep on the grass, wrapped in the warm blankets. Soon, it would grow dark, but for a little while at least, they could let the girls rest before putting them on the horses for the trek down the mountain.

Turning to Jake, Josie said softly, "Thank you for coming." They listened to Star and Robin's steady breathing and the occasional snore. "I had no rope, and I'm not good with heights. I'm not even upset you brought Blue."

"Blue? You mean, Tornado?" Jake placed his hand over hers, covering it with his warmth. "Why do I have a feeling I'm going to have to change the name of my horse?"

"My horse," she replied, her tone still soft, but a coy smile appearing on her face as she withdrew her hand from beneath his strong, warm one. As much as she wanted to keep her hand safe under his, the subject of their conversation still irritated her, but perhaps not as much as before.

"Tell me about your mare," he said as they looked out from the mountain, enjoying the view of Honey River Canyon spread out below. They could see the church steeple jutting above the rooftops of many of the homes and businesses, and dirt roads leading to the countryside where patches of meadows, wooded areas, and the occasional barn dotted the scenery.

"Mrs. Velvet is a rescue horse, much like these darlings," she answered as they studied the town. "A wild mustang, and unusual for her solid black coat, she had become tangled in a bramble. Her legs were infected from fighting her way out. She had scrapes and cuts everywhere, but especially on her legs. I found her trying to lick and tend her wounds under a shady tree not far from the bramble. She let me put a lead on her, and I brought her home where Pa and I nursed her back to health. Pa said she'd always be my horse and would make a fine start to our future horse farm. Since he passed, it's been our goal to honor his memory by turning Cherry Crossing into not only a thriving cherry and apple orchard on what is primarily a wheat farm, but also a thriving horse farm."

"How is it going? I mean, you have other horses, I noticed."

Jake traced one of her hands with his index finger, drawing her attention as they observed the differences between his larger hands and her smaller, delicate ones.

"We have our first foal. He'll be a colt by summer. We've named him Gallant. His mother is Violet, and his father is Chicory, a fine quarter horse, but not as nice as Blue. Violet is our best broodmare, but Vera could be one, too. They are our chestnut mares, and they were among the first horses Pa bought here in Montana. Chicory is our only stallion until Gallant grows up, and although he's a wonderful plowing horse, he's brown and white. He isn't good enough to fetch a fine price, but the foal is beautiful. Violet and Vera are our only matching team, so you see, Blue will make a fine mate for Mrs. Velvet, and then we'll have more foals to build our farm, to honor Pa's dream."

"Is it your dream? Is it what you want to do? You and your sisters?" he asked. "I assume the three of you own the farm together?"

She nodded. "Yes, we share it equally. It's not our only dream, but it's one of the biggest. Jillian wants to become a teacher to buy more horses; and Jackie wants to marry someone wealthy, have beautiful dresses, and buy more horses, so she takes in extra sewing. I teach at the mission and help in many other ways toward the end of purchasing more horses. Someday I guess we shall all three settle down and have families of our own, but I suppose there will be plenty of time for those dreams, too."

"Tell me about the mission," he prodded.

"The mission. Well, I'll try. As I understand it, the mission is a converging of great minds from several dioceses in the Western

Hemisphere. They wanted to be a part of spreading the gospel in the westward expansion of the United States. Their leaders have kept in touch through letters, and they sent volunteers who felt called to this area to establish a mission here," she explained. "It wasn't here when I arrived with my family. I was only eight years old then. About the time of my tenth birthday—the age Robin is now—Padre Cornelius arrived from one of the oldest missions in the U.S., in St. Augustine, Florida. He is from Ireland and speaks with an Irish brogue. In fact, he loves Charles Dickens books. His mother was from England, but his father was a sheep farmer from Ireland. It's where he grew up, in Ireland, herding sheep. I heard him deliver a sermon once and he said he changed his name at the St. Augustine to reflect the deep work the Lord had done in his heart there. I'm not sure why he chose Cornelius. Perhaps the name belonged to someone who influenced him to become a priest in Ireland as I believe it is a very Irish sort of name."

"Sheep herding is an excellent background for a priest." Jake plucked a sturdy strand appearing to be something akin to wild hay from the grassy area around them. He chewed on it, thinking about all she'd relayed. "Where did the other nuns and priests come from?"

Josie couldn't help but wonder if Jake felt ready to confide in her what he'd shared with Mother Marta, about being a minister. Since he didn't yet, she continued, figuring he would tell her in time.

"Bishop Thomas has the most interesting background. He came from the Diocese of Puerto Rico. He has a long thin nose and is very tan. His country of origin is England, but his mother was Puerto Rican. He speaks Spanish, but he is good with teaching English grammar, spelling, and cursive writing because his father, an Englishman, loved literature and passed this love on to him."

"I see. Are there any other priests here?" he asked.

"No, just those two. As for the nuns, Sister Francesca is a Roman Catholic transplant from the Diocese of New Orleans, and later, the Diocese of Oregon City. She came here from Oregon, but she speaks fondly of the beauty of the St. Louis Cathedral. I believe it must be very grand.

"Sister Angel, she's from Maryland, but she came here from a Catholic Mission in Atlanta, Georgia. She is deathly afraid of insects, and I'm concerned about her because her spectacles are broken. She can hardly see where she is going half the time. Sister Agnes is hard of hearing, and she came with Mother Marta from Cincinnati where they both taught in a parochial school. Agnes and Angel were both orphans at one time, so they are particularly good with the children, but they are elderly now, so it is very hard work for them to help at the mission. Nonetheless, I discovered they have committed to a lifetime of service to the work of the Lord as nuns, and I admire their devotion greatly. It inspires me."

"Do you want to become a nun?" he asked, turning to look at her.

Josie laughed. "Oh, no, never! I could never become a nun. I like kissing too much, and nuns can never marry. How can one know they will never marry? What if they meet someone and fall in love? Think of the misery of having to be kept apart or break their vows or whatever it is they say when they become nuns or priests! Besides, I can be downright obstinate and outspoken at times. I don't mind helping at the mission, but I'll never be as good as they are."

Jake chuckled, nodding. "I'll never be as good as they are, either. In fact, according to God's Word, we are only made clean by the sprinkling of the blood of the Lamb who was slain for our sins. We'd never be good enough no matter what we do, except for the fact the Lord Jesus died for us."

Josie took in his words, glad to hear them. She had accepted Jesus as her Savior because of what He'd done for her on the cross. To hear Jake explain it so simply, even a child could understand.

He continued, "Of course, we do have to set our sails toward holiness and living the Christian life to follow Jesus. It is a life of discipline and devotion. Not for the faint of heart." Then he stopped. "Ach, do I sound like I'm preaching?"

"No. Not at all. You're very gifted. Your words have me mesmerized. I want to write them down," she admitted.

"I spent years studying theology at a school in Philadelphia with Hugh. I obtained my preaching certificate there and became an assistant pastor for four years at a church of the same denomination as the one here in Honey River Canyon," he explained. "But none of this means I don't want to kiss you every time I see you." Jake leaned in closer to her, kissing her again, sending tingles of joy up her spine.

Then he pulled away. "Now, I've divulged too much, and yet not enough. The truth is, I punched someone, and it led to my being asked to step down, but the fellow deserved it. In fact, I'd probably do it again."

"Don't worry," she laughed, trying to picture him punching someone. "I'm not a gossip, and I can see the need to let people get to know you for you. If the man deserved it, you have nothing to fear, except maybe not turning the other cheek. I faulter there, too."

"You're right. The Bible does instruct us to turn the other cheek, and not to display anger. Since we're talking about things, I want you to know I didn't have anything to do with what happened to Chad," he said.

"I know." She nodded, touching his jaw for a moment. "I believe you."

Jake didn't say anything more for a while, but Josie noticed he seemed to relax a whole lot more after their conversation as tension drained from him. After a while, he stretched and then stood, helping her up from the ground. "We should get going if we're going to make it to the mission before dark. I'm sure Mother Marta is anxious."

She agreed with him. Nightfall would come soon enough. They'd barely make it down the mountain before dark. "Yes, we'll let them sleep in our arms as we ride down the mountain. I'm looking forward to a hot bath and sleep when I reach home. We'd best get a move on." Josie began gathering their belongings, thankful for the Lord's help in the rescue, and the time she'd shared with Jake.

He surprised her as she fussed with tightening Mrs. Violet's saddle and adjusting her saddle blanket, pulling her toward him one last time before they woke the girls, brushing her lips with a soft and gentle kiss as he held an arm around her waist. How the man stirred her! She melted in his embrace, wondering if she should flee as she pushed him away, hiding a coy smile from him under the brim of her bonnet. Surely, he would not toy with her feelings. Surely, he meant something with his flirtatious and forward kissing which left her wanting more. Surely, he would soon make his intentions known. Wouldn't he?

Then again, perhaps he had quite a lot on his plate with clearing his name and running for mayor. Maybe she should try to take things one day at a time. Accustomed to her independence, if the idea of moving too fast caused her a brief desire to flee at times, could it do the same to Jake? Yes, they should take it slow.

Chapter Twenty

"For I know the plans I have for you," declares the Lord, "plans to prosper you and not to harm you, plans to give you a hope and a future."

Jeremiah 29:11, NIV

Sheriff Casey Drummond arrived on the stoop to the cabin at Cherry Crossing Farmstead and would have knocked, but he saw a note on the door attached by a generous dab of tree sap which read, *Dear Josie, Jackie and I have gone to the mission with some cherry scones to comfort the nuns. We hope to meet you there when you find Robin and Star. Affectionately yours, Jillian.*

He turned around and took off his hat, raking a hand through his hair before returning it to his head. Between the missing orphans Padre Cornelius had reported, and the death of Joshua Martin's eldest, he didn't have much time for wild goose chases. He'd ridden all the way out to the Hayes farm for two reasons. One, he'd hoped to find the orphans had turned up there since he'd heard of their fondness for Jocelyn, and secondly, to follow up on one of the suspicious new characters in town who'd escorted the middle Hayes sister to the spring dance.

He didn't trust new folks, and the milliner had mentioned something about the fellow which just plain didn't sit right with him. She'd said Miss Jacqueline had seemed in a hurry to find him on the night of the dance. While he had the utmost of respect for the Hayes sisters and all they'd done to work their farm after the loss of their parents, he hoped they would not become tangled up with someone sinister.

Now he'd have to return out here some other time. He had asked Hattie Pierson, the town librarian, to dine at Anne's Kitchen and accompany him to see a play at Sarah Campbell's Theater. He'd best not turn up late, or she'd think him rude, and he liked Hattie a whole lot. One man could only do so much. This week, he had enough work to keep him busy day and night, and no deputy to assist unless he deputized someone. Maybe first thing tomorrow, he'd deputize someone, if he could figure out an ideal sort of candidate.

Jake sank into the hot bath the housekeeper had prepared for him while he'd eaten his evening meal in the dining room with Hugh. Unfortunately, Hugh's errand to find the waif-like creature had turned up emptyhanded. At least they'd rescued the orphans, and his belligerent beauty had not scolded him once. The folks at the mission had swarmed them outside before he and Jocelyn had even dismounted. Jillian had offered them cherry scones to tide them over until they could return home for dinner, although the nuns had tried to persuade them to join them for a celebration meal. They'd settled on tea and some of those delicious scones the Hayes sisters had made from Cherry Crossing's preserves, but he'd felt compelled to accompany Josie and her sisters to their cabin door afterward. Strange things had happened in Honey River Canyon since he'd arrived, and he had no intention of letting his guard down.

The orphan girls had learned a hard lesson about the dangers of running away, and except for Chad's funeral to attend tomorrow, perhaps he could finally turn his attention to clearing his name. Hugh had said he'd covered a lot of territory, but more doors remained to knock on. Why did God answer some prayers, and not others? Hadn't he prayed, asking God to bless Hugh's efforts? He pondered the matter heavily. How could he become a preacher or give hope to others about the Lord if he couldn't even explain why God didn't answer some prayers right away, and others, He answered relatively quickly?

Did it come down to the Lord developing patience within a man? Or did God not answer some prayers because He had to test one's faith? He had to conclude each situation varied, and perhaps no cut and dried answer could prevail over any others, but finding patience and enduring faithfulness in times of testing surely aggravated him.

What if they couldn't clear his name? What then? Sheriff Drummond had said the only reason he wouldn't arrest him had to do with Jake's grandparents, and the note. Things could be worse. He could be sitting in a cold jail cell, isolated from the world, unable to participate in clearing his name.

Exhausted, Jake went to bed, thinking he'd fall asleep in minutes after the physically strenuous day of riding up and down a steep mountain, crossing the town to opposite ends of the countryside twice, and the emotional toil of the rescue and the delay in searching for the one person who might help him clear his name. Instead, he tossed and turned, his soul a mixture of despair and hope in the bedroom once belonging to his brave, heroic grandfather.

Tossing the covers aside, he rose from his attempt to slumber, pacing the floor over a patch of moonlight streaming through one of the windows facing the town. He found himself still wrestling with the fact the Lord hadn't answered the total sum of his prayer by blessing Hugh's efforts, and yet he'd set aside his agenda to help the orphan girls, and to attend church on Sunday, respecting the day as the Lord's Day for worship and rest. Now, he found himself angry, wanting to lash out at God because of his predicament. An accusation of murder was serious indeed! He'd heard of men hanging for lesser crimes. He needed God's help in a desperate way.

He had to find his confidence and trust in the Lord, the one who'd always been his mainstay, his refuge in times of trouble. He had to find it not only for himself, but to possess the ability to share the gospel and faith. Yet, this did not seem right when one considered the plight of Paul who wrote the epistles from a prison in Rome, or John the Baptist, beheaded for preaching repentance and the need for baptism. The disciples had suffered for the Lord, and countless others. They'd stoned Stephen, and

Jesus himself had suffered the crucifixion. The question became, did God truly expect or ask this same kind of devotion to him in this time, in this place, in this battle?

As he dug deeper still in his thoughts and prayers, Jake thought of King David, the one who'd penned the Psalms, the apple of God's eye, a man who thirsted after the presence of God. What did David do but encourage himself in the Lord, and continually trust in the Lord, and cry out to Him in times of trouble. There, Jake found himself, crying out to the Lord in his distress and anguish of soul. He could not fathom a God who had brought him this far west to hang for a murder he did not commit, not when everything lay at his feet and within his reach for a good future—one which might even include the beautiful Josie at his side. Did not God promise He had good plans and a good future for him in Jeremiah?

Hope rose with the dawn of first light the more fervently he prayed, reciting the Scriptures he'd stored in his heart. He would cling to the goodness of the Father, the mercy of the Lord, trusting He had not yet finished answering his prayer. Perhaps the houses and establishments Hugh had visited brought him one step closer, and they would not have to visit those again. They could cross those off the list, and this had indeed made the day a success. He must cling to the belief God planned to clear his name, and no weapon formed against him would prosper. However, one thing became clear. *He* had to wield the sword, the Word of the Lord, and speak it out loud, believing it by faith.

After he spoke the Scriptures out loud, his soul knew the joy of refreshing, restoration of hope, and assurance of victory deep down inside. He could rest now, at least for a few hours, having unleashed God's Word and his faith. His God would not let him down, and He would one day impart these keys to someone else in need of the reminder of the nature of the God of Israel and His lovingkindness. God did not require everyone to become martyrs of the faith.

Chapter Twenty-One

Let love and faithfulness never leave you; bind them around
your neck, write them on the tablet of your heart. Then you
will win favor and a good name in the sight of God and man.

Proverbs 3:3-4, NIV

"Hello Mother Marta. What brings you to town this morning?"
Twila Thornton looked up from behind her printing press as
the nun entered her establishment. "I thought you'd be
attending Chad's funeral with everyone else. In fact, Sheldon
went on our behalf. I'm still too upset about his death to
attend, or I'd be there myself."

Marta tossed a copy of last Sunday's newspaper carrying the
story of Jake's accusation onto the counter, and Twila stepped

over to it to have a closer look at which words Marta's bony finger pointed to on the printed page.

"It's just news, Mother Marta, nothing more. The public deserves to know what's at stake here. Jacob Hunter is a newcomer to town, even if his grandfather was an honorable man. He might not be anything like the colonel. We don't really know, and my job is to print the news." Twila smoothed her dark blue work apron out over the black mourning dress she wore. Marta guessed the dark apron hid some of the ink stains Twila acquired from working the press.

She crossed her arms over the metal cross necklace dangling over her habit. "Twila, I'm bringing you a new story, and I want you to promise me you'll print a special edition. It's newsworthy, and it needs to go out right away. It involves this man. He's a hero, just like his grandfather, and the town deserves to know the truth about his character."

Twila sounded hesitant. She tilted her head to one side, a doubtful look appearing in her eyes. "I don't know. It depends on the story. Tell me more, and I'll talk to Sheldon. My husband is editor in chief, and we usually decide things like this together. Ink is expensive, and we'll have to fill at least a whole page to be able to justify a special edition, preferably front and back."

Marta finished relaying her story about Jake's courageous act of heroism in rescuing the missing orphans to Mrs. Thornton, and before leaving, she'd obtained a promise to work something up as soon as possible. Twila even thanked her for coming over straightaway.

"Does anyone else know about this yet?" Twila asked as Marta turned to go.

"No, only the mission staff and children, and the Hayes

sisters, and maybe Jake's household know about it. I was going to notify the sheriff so he could stop searching and focus on finding the real murderer, but thinking about it, he might be attending the funeral. I'm needed at the mission, or I'd attend the funeral too, but with Josie off today, and the emotional turmoil we went through while the girls were missing, I don't think my nerves could handle a funeral, too." Marta paused in case Twila needed to ask anything else, adding, "Oh, and it's possible a few folks might know because Padre Cornelius and Bishop Thomas conducted a search on Sunday afternoon in an effort to find the girls, and they continued on Monday."

"Thank you. We'll still run it. I'm not sure how soon we can have it ready, but I'll get to work on it. I'm sure Sheldon will approve. This is big news, and it certainly does shed light on Jacob Hunter's character. It's hard to think of someone like him capable of..." Twila Thornton started to choke up as tears filled her eyes.

Marta nodded. "I couldn't agree more. Thank you again, Twila. I very much look forward to this edition, and I think it will be a sensation. Townsfolk will appreciate the *Honey River Gazette*. I'm sure they're torn and confused, but this story shows us a glimpse of truth we desperately need right now."

She pushed the door open and slipped outside to the buggy, thankful the Lord worked in mysterious ways, and sometimes she appreciated the fact He allowed her to participate in the revelation of truth. The very idea Jake Hunter could have hurt anyone made her want to tip over some tables in the marketplace like Jesus. She snapped the reins after climbing into the conveyance, hoping she'd at least tipped the balance in Jake's favor.

After attending Chad's home-going service with her sisters, Josie's nerves wanted to explode as Jillian steered the wagon home in silence, thankful her youngest sister had insisted on driving. "You're in no condition to drive," Jillian had said, pointing to the passenger seat. "Jacqueline has offered to sit in the back, and here, take my extra handkerchief. Blow your nose. You sniffled all through the last half an hour. Dry your tears, and before long, we'll be at our cabin with a cup of tea and a hot meal. The pot roast and vegetables are perfectly tender. All we need do is warm it up a bit."

Josie hadn't found the strength to argue with her. She'd only nodded silently to all Jillian said and climbed into the passenger seat, thinking Jake and Hugh had displayed good sense in not attending the service. It would only have aggravated Joshua and Charlie Martin. They'd now helped the family lay a good friend to rest. As the wagon rumbled its way home, she prayed Chad might make it into heaven for the first time since his passing, berating herself for not having prayed it sooner.

Josie began to recover from her grief and the stares some of the townsfolk had given her as she enjoyed a cup of steaming hot tea flavored with apples and cinnamon, picking at the roast, carrots, and potatoes on the plate before her for lack of an appetite. She supposed people wondered why she'd never married Chad, and if Jake and Chad had argued over her like Joshua had said. Her cheeks had burned red at the thought of it all, but she'd held her chin up and tried to ignore their whispers and curious looks. Oddly enough, she struggled with her feelings of guilt and remorse for not loving Chad enough to marry him. She told herself she needn't add their expectations to her plate.

Since Jackie remained oddly silent again, as she had ever since the dance, Jillian occasionally carried on little bits of conversation for them. "What do you think of these new square sugar cubes? They've finally made their way to Montana Territory. I rather like them; except they don't melt as quickly. I like the way they look in the sugar bowl, and they are nice for measuring out the right amount of sugar for tea or coffee. Not so good for cooking and baking, though. Katy Emmerson highly recommended them."

"Yes, I like them too, just like these new four-tined silver forks, and the can openers. Ma would rejoice over these can openers with little cutting wheels and the new forks." Josie held up her fork and stared at it. No more eating from narrow, sharp knives.

Glancing at Jackie, she noticed her picking at her food, as well. Perhaps she sulked because Abel hadn't called on her since the dance. She did offer to help Jill wash the dishes so Josie could do as she pleased.

Restless, Josie wandered about the front room, straightening the room a bit by fluffing pillows, folding lap blankets, and stacking books. She finally sat down at Ma's piano in the front room, wondering what to play. She leafed through the one hymnal they owned and the sheets of music they'd collected over the years. She finally chose "What a Friend We Have in Jesus." She played the first verse one time through without singing the lines. Then she repeated it, singing the words ever so gently, her voice exquisite. Before long, both of her sisters entered from the kitchen and sat down near the fireplace to listen.

When she finished the piece, she burst into tears. Jill rose from one of the parlor benches and placed a comforting hand on her shoulder. "What is it, Josie? I know you didn't love Chad. Is he why you're crying?"

"Partly," Josie sniffled. "And partly because the man I do love is in so much trouble for something he didn't do. He doesn't deserve to suffer like this when we have finally found each other." She sighed. "It seems as if our chances for happiness are to be snuffed out like a candle before we have a chance to begin." She buried her face in her hands. "And I can't help but remember flashbacks of the kind childhood friend we had in Chad. I see his boyhood face with his smile and laughter every now and then. It pains me so to think someone has murdered him. Although I didn't want to marry him, he didn't deserve to be murdered, and I know the man I love didn't do it."

Jillian listened, ever the gentle soul, and even Jacqueline, usually a chatterbox, didn't interrupt. Josie rose from the piano, closing the lid over the keys. "I think I shall write an entry in my journal and then rest for a while, and when I'm rested, I may ride out to the mission to see how Robin and Star have recovered. I can't sit around here waiting for the hay to grow."

"I think you have a good plan. Rest always makes me feel better. There's something healing about it. And Jocelyn, don't give up. Truth and justice will prevail," her youngest sister offered. "I just keep imagining the same face you described, only now he's in heaven, playing in heavenly fields and meadows, with Jesus."

"Thank you, Jillian. Such a beautiful and comforting thought. I shall try very hard to think of him in the meadows with Jesus." Josie crossed the cabin to the staircase, glancing at Jacqueline on her right as she passed through the cabin toward the staircase. Pa had built it against the far wall of the dining area where Ma had usually served their dinner meals at the table in the front room. Her middle sister, seated on one of the parlor benches by the fireplace with a knee tucked under her, had crease lines in her forehead revealing deep thought activity, and stunned, troubled eyes. The events of the last few days had obviously taken a toll on all three of them.

She paused on the third step. "Are you all right, Jackie? You've been so quiet these past few days."

Jackie bit her lip and nodded. "I'm... I'm fine. It's just everything, I guess. It's all so disturbing."

Josie nodded and climbed the steps. What else could she say? She felt the same way.

Chapter Twenty-Two

Ask and it will be given to you; seek and you will find; knock
and the door will be opened to you.

Mathew 7:7, NIV

"Arthur, we need your help." Jake leaned against the butler's pantry counter, his arms crossed over his chest. Hugh stood by in the background as Jake continued to explain his situation, one he knew Arthur Penworth likely already knew from reading the newspaper and hearing the local town gossip. "We don't know the people of Honey River Canyon well enough to approach them and gain their trust to ask even the simplest of questions, and if we don't find the girl who handed me this note, we have little hope of clearing my name from the murder of Chad Martin."

Arthur nodded, moving away from the stack of dishes he planned to put away into their proper places. "I understand. You can count on me. What would you like me to do, sir?"

"We'll need you to ride with us and introduce us to folks as we finish canvasing the area. Folks will be returning to their homes since the funeral is over. It's a good time to finish our search," Jake said. "We're looking for families who might have a teenage girl about the age of sixteen or seventeen living with them. Brown hair, brown eyes, about five feet, on the small side."

Arthur tilted his head as he considered the description. "I suppose this narrows it some. Shall we discuss the farms and homes you've already spoken to after we saddle up some horses?"

"Good plan," Jake agreed. The three of them headed to the stables after Arthur had a brief word with Maddie to let her know Tolliver should oversee the male employed servants in his absence.

Half an hour later, Arthur had narrowed their search down to three families who lived south of town. The Nelson family had a fourteen-year-old daughter, Betsy, who might look about sixteen. The Sumner and Harris families also had daughters who fit Jake's description, Lilah Sumner and Ellie Harris. They rode out to the Sumner farm first, but after Arthur introduced Jake and Hugh to Mrs. Sumner, and they'd met Lilah, Jake knew this young lady wasn't the one who'd handed him the note.

Next, they passed the Wiley farm until reaching the neighboring farm owned by the Harris family. They dismounted, and Arthur led them to the shanty door, introducing Jake and

Hugh to Mrs. Harris, who invited them to step inside. She seemed to know and respect Arthur, at least a little. After chatting about the approach of summer and the rainy spring, Arthur let Jake do the talking, stepping aside.

Jake recognized the cloak hanging in a front corner from some pegs as he looked around, his gaze returning to the children clinging to and around their mother's skirt. They stared up at him with curious, large eyes.

"We're looking for a young lady who attended the dance with brown hair, maybe brown eyes, not very tall, but she wore a cloak, resembling the one hanging over there." He motioned toward a cloak he saw hanging on a peg, trying to keep things simple with his explanation, but he didn't see a girl matching the description among them. He only saw many small children swarming around their mother. Perhaps an elder daughter hid in the other room of the shanty.

"Brown hair, possibly brown eyes, not too tall, and wearing a cloak like the one hanging right there?" Mrs. Harris repeated as she looked Jake over, nodding toward the cloak hanging from a row of pegs on the wall amongst shawls, wraps, aprons, and coats in many sizes, colors, and fabrics.

Jake nodded as she balanced a baby on her hip who let out a wail. He looked like a boy, and a cute little one with his straight blond hair and big blue eyes.

"And she isn't in any kind of trouble?" the woman asked as she reached for a rattle on the table and placed it in the baby's hand. The child gripped it and cooed, temporarily satisfied.

"No ma'am, no trouble. We'd only like to have a word with her and ask a few questions about someone she might be able to help us find. Can you tell us where she might be? It's a matter of utmost urgency." Jake shifted his weight to his other leg and looked around the two rooms of the shanty, his eyes returning to the dark cloak near the door. Hugh remained silent behind him as their eyes adjusted to the dim light of the shanty. It had only one window, and the crisp white curtains shut out much of the light.

"It does sound as if you've described my Ellie," Mrs. Harris commented reluctantly, "and we did give her permission to stop in at the dance with a friend if she promised not to stay for too long. George and I didn't go. I didn't want to saddle Ellie with the children. George, Junior and his brothers here, Oliver, Henry, and Arthur, can be a handful. Plus, baby Miles. Molly and Mavis can be helpful, but they have their moments."

Millicent Harris spoke true words. Far too many children existed in the small space, but what Jake did see appeared clean and tidy. He counted four boys and two girls, most appearing under the age of seven he guessed. A table with benches took up most of the space. He took note of one cookstove to heat both rooms. It occupied the corner of the far wall, and a cupboard stood beside it. Two rocking chairs were drawn up to the cook-stove for warmth. Across from the table, he saw a bed in the front room with privacy curtains closed around most of it. These items left barely enough room for anyone to move around.

A glance toward the other room and he thought perhaps it contained one or more beds, but judging from the size of the shanty, he guessed two beds at most, and maybe a trundle bed. A curtain covered most of the door to the bedroom, but he could see a patchwork quilt on the bed like the quilt on the one in the front room. It all appeared cozy, but so crowded.

"You have a beautiful family, ma'am," Jake replied. He could tell she wanted to keep talking to feel safe enough to divulge any information to him. Likely, her husband had gone into town looking for extra work, or perhaps he worked in the fields at this moment.

"Thank you. Well, I can tell you Ellie is a nice girl, and her pa and I don't want any trouble."

"No trouble," he repeated.

Mrs. Harris sighed, a look in her eyes of distrust as she relented to telling him more. "We aren't Catholic, but we gave her our permission to seek employment for extra wages at the mission. She has seemed a little troubled about something or other lately, as if something is distracting her. I think it might be good for her to get away from all the little ones. She's always helping with the cooking, cleaning, the children, doing extra chores for us. Works too hard that one. Studious too, as much as she can be. I worry about her, but she generally does every-thing we ask. Has never given us one bit of trouble. Always does her homework."

"So, Ellie is on her way to the mission," Jake repeated. "Do you know when she left? I assume she set out on foot?"

Ellie's mother nodded. "Yes, she set out on foot after school, about half an hour ago. She's most likely nearly there. If you hurry, mayhap you can catch up with her."

"Thank you kindly, ma'am." Jake handed her some green-backs from his wallet. "Please, take it for the family for some-thing you need. I appreciate the help. It's the least I can do."

Before she could decline the cash, Arthur, Jake, and Hugh left her at the door wondering about the exact reason for their business as they hurried to their horses, anxious to make it to the mission and find Ellie. Finally, the breakthrough they'd waited for. Jake breathed a small sigh of relief, hopeful as he swung up into the saddle. *Thank you, Lord.*

Jake urged his stallion to follow the others, and soon they picked up the pace from a trot to a gallop toward the mission. Ellie remained their only lead, and they couldn't take any chances on missing her.

Arthur, Jake, and Hugh filed inside the mission, intent on finding the girl, removing their hats as they entered. Sister Angel waved to them as she passed through the main hall, helping them to not feel like intruders. She smiled and kept going in the direction of the chapel, apparently remembering Jake had delivered Robin and Star safely only the night before. They'd had tea in the dining hall. He took the lead and Arthur and Hugh followed when he turned right to enter the dining hall once again. To his surprise, they found Ellie at once. She sat at the end of one of the long tables near the entrance, perhaps waiting to speak with Mother Marta or some other senior staff member about employment.

Jake recognized her as soon as they entered the long dining room from the main entrance hall. "There she is!" he whispered to Hugh and Arthur. "She's the waif who gave me the note."

A few children wandered in and out from the opposite end of the hall, but Ellie didn't seem to know any of them or speak to anyone else. Jake had also noticed Josie's mare tethered to the hitching post out front, but finding her would have to wait for the moment. He nodded at Arthur, who stepped forward to address Ellie before they lost the opportunity.

"Miss Harris," Arthur began, "I presume you remember the colonel, our former mayor."

"Hello, Mr. Penworth. I do." Ellie nodded in the affirmative, and Jake thanked the Lord she recognized his trusted butler.

Arthur continued, extending an arm to introduce Jake and Hugh. "His grandson, Mr. Jacob Hunter, and his friend, Hugh Stanton, are with me. They would like to ask you a few important questions about the night of the dance, if you don't mind."

Ellie didn't protest, and Jake immediately stepped a little closer, withdrawing the note from inside his suit coat pocket. "Let's start at the beginning. When you gave me this note that evening, it is my belief you did not write it. I believe someone asked you to hand it to me. Can you tell me if I am correct, or did you perhaps write this note?"

Ellie looked at Arthur as if deciding whether she could trust any of them. She bit her lower lip. "I did not write it. I'm not even sure what it says. I didn't read it. I was only asked to deliver the note within ten minutes of receiving it. The man offered to pay me handsomely, and he said it would be in my best interest to immediately leave the premises after doing so."

"How much did he offer you to deliver the note?" Hugh asked from where he stood slightly behind Arthur.

"He gave me five dollars, and I did what he asked. Then I left." Ellie bit her lip again, looking around the room nervously. "Did I do anything wrong?"

"No, Ellie. You didn't do anything wrong exactly. The man

who gave you this note may have done something wrong. Can you tell us his name, or anything at all about the individual?"

"Oh, yes, let me see if I can remember..." Ellie's brows furrowed. "Oh yes, he had a slight scar above his left eye. It's not a long scar, but maybe an inch long."

Jake glanced over his shoulder when he heard the rustle of skirts, aware of Mother Marta drawing near, standing quietly behind them. Looking to his left at some other commotion, he saw Josie enter the long room carrying a tray with some activity for Robin, Star, and some other children following her. Jake saw her nod and smile in his direction as she set the tray on the far end of the same table where Ellie sat. The children swarmed around the tray, presumably about to make something from colorful beads in the bowls he could now see.

Ellie began to divulge more information, causing him to return his attention to her. "Now I do recall his name. It was Abel. I heard the other man step up to his side and call him Abel when he told him to hurry up and have the note delivered. It all seemed rather odd to me, but I needed the cash. I don't know what any of it meant. I'm not in any trouble, am I?" Ellie's eyes looked from Jake to Arthur, and then to Hugh, back to Jake again.

"No, you're not in any trouble," Jake replied. "You've been most helpful." He didn't remember having much chance to speak to the fellow who'd escorted the middle Hayes sister to the dance, but he recalled the name.

At this moment, Miss Jacqueline Hayes flew around the corner from the main entrance hall, nearly bumping into Mother Marta. She looked agitated as she glanced around the room as if looking for someone. Spying Josie, she picked up her skirt, and stepped around them to speak with her sister, whispering something in her ear. Jake noticed Josie's mouth drop open in response, and she turned immediately to look toward him. Why did he have a feeling whatever Jacqueline had whispered had something to do with him?

Jake turned his attention back to Ellie again. "Thank you so much for telling us what you do remember. It's all we needed to know, Miss Harris. I believe you're here to speak to Mother Marta. We won't trouble you any further." Jake folded the note and returned it to the pocket inside his suit coat, stepping aside with Hugh and Arthur so the Mother Superior could speak to Ellie.

"If you'll follow me, Miss Harris, Padre Cornelius will speak to you in the chapel," Mother Marta said. Ellie nodded and rose to follow the nun's instruction.

Closer to knowing who'd killed Chad, Jake met Josie and her sister in the middle of the room, Hugh and Arthur on his heels. Before he could say anything however, Robin spotted his presence.

"Mister Jake!" Robin jumped up from her seat to give him a hug. Star followed, equally happy to see him.

Jake knelt and gave each Indian girl a hug, tugging on one of Robin's braids, which made her laugh. "You both look so well. You are home, rested, safe at last, never to run away again." The girls nodded, smiling.

"We promise we won't run away ever again," Robin assured him. She made the sign of the cross over herself.

"We promise," Star agreed, crossing her heart. "It was so scary! Our mountain climbing days are over before they could ever begin."

Jake laughed, and the girls returned to their seats at the table with their friends from the mission, other orphans who looked thankful to have the girls in their midst once again. He noticed they looked warm, freshly bathed, fed, loved, and happy. He also noticed the joy in their eyes at having a safe environment.

"Girls, please continue making the beaded necklaces while I speak to my friends and sister," Josie explained to the orphans as Jake noticed her sister, Miss Jacqueline, standing by twisting a handkerchief repeatedly in her gloved hands. Josie turned to Jake and her sister, lowering her voice. "My sister said since you are here, you'll want to hear what she has to say. May I suggest we speak in the kitchen? Most of the students are either here in the dining hall or the great parlor, but we might have a little privacy in the kitchen if you'll follow me. Sister Francesca and Sister Agnes are in the kitchen, but they can be trusted. Hugh and Arthur may come along, too. Ah, here is Sister Angel. She can stay with the children while we talk."

Sister Angel nodded and waved them away as she sat down with the children. Mother Marta returned in time to hear Jake say, "The kitchen will be fine."

They followed Jocelyn into the kitchen. He'd never seen much of the interior of the mission beyond the dining hall, and Jake found himself enjoying the stone floors, large brick fireplaces, and seeing everything organized and stowed properly in its place. The smell of something delicious wafted in the air, and he dismissed the growling in his belly, reminding him the dinner hour grew near.

In the kitchen, he noticed several worktables in the middle, another large brick fireplace, and a large pantry lined with jars of jams, jellies, garden veggies, corn relish, and other supplies.

Drying herbs, stock pots, and pans of all sizes hung from the ceiling. Shelving and cupboards housed dishes and other necessary items. The large cookstove, polished to a gleaming black, took up twice the space of the one in his own kitchen.

Mother Marta caught sight of him looking around, taking everything in. "You may not know this, Jacob, but your grandfather, Colonel Bradshaw, funded much of our building when we first arrived. I'd guess Josie was only about ten years old when we established St. Paul's Mission. He and Mrs. Bradshaw donated the new cookstove a few years ago."

"I had no idea," Jake replied, continually amazed at the things he learned about his grandfather—and Josie, too. "I have so much to live up to."

Sister Francesca and Sister Agnes nodded at everyone from the farthest worktable, but they continued their work making cornmeal muffins for the next morning's breakfast while a large kettle of beef stew for the children's supper simmered in the kitchen fireplace. Jake couldn't help his eyes returning to the stew once he realized what smelled so good.

"Now that we are here," Josie began as they crowded around the empty worktable, "my sister, Jacqueline, has something important to share. Do bear in mind there are children and priests who sometimes roam through the kitchen from the dining hall and the great parlor." She motioned to the room on the other side of the kitchen. "All right, Jackie. Tell us why you came all this way. What's happening? And what does this have to do with Jake?"

Chapter Twenty-Three

Be strong and courageous. Do not be afraid or terrified because of them, for the Lord your God goes with you; He will never leave you nor forsake you.

Deuteronomy 31:6, NIV

Jacqueline had tears in her eyes, but Jocelyn reached across the table, squeezing her sister's hand gently to give her courage when she only released a hiccup at first. Then she plunged forward, looking at Jacob Hunter, Arthur Penworth, and then Hugh Stanton. "Jake, I didn't expect to find you here with Arthur and Hugh. I'm terribly glad you're here though, because I'm hoping you'll all know what to do. We're going to need protection. I came here to speak to Josie first because I couldn't wait until she returned home. One more day, and who knows if I'll even be alive."

"What's this about, exactly?" Josie asked. "Why do you question if you'll be alive?"

"Abel Keller," Jackie replied, dabbing the corners of her eyes with a handkerchief trimmed in fine crocheted tatting. "He killed Chad Martin the night of the dance. I saw the whole thing, but he threatened to kill me too if I told anyone. He's been riding out to our farm every night since the dance, sitting outside on his horse, watching us, waiting for me to come outside. I'm terrified to go anywhere alone. I barely escaped him to come here this evening, but Jillian is outside in the wagon, keeping an eye out for him with a shotgun in case he followed us. We think we left in time for him not to see us, but we aren't sure."

"Jillian is outside with a shotgun?" Hugh repeated, his brow rising as he stepped toward the kitchen window to peer outside. He parted the kitchen curtain a little more to open up the view. "She sure is."

"Don't worry. Our Pa taught us how to shoot as well as anybody," Josie said without looking at Hugh. She kept her eyes riveted on Jackie. "I thought something happened when Abel drove you home earlier than the rest of us. I kept thinking you must have been ill or worn yourself out. But why? Why would he kill Chad?"

"I was sick all right—sick to my stomach from what I saw." Jackie sniffled, dabbing her eyes with the handkerchief, and removing her gloves.

"Before we get to the why part of what Chad did, tell us

exactly what you saw, Miss Hayes." Jake crossed his arms over his chest, but his voice remained calm and reassuring.

"At one point on the night of the dance, I couldn't find Abel, and he'd already missed a reel or two, so I went outside to the courtyard, hoping to find him. I only ran into the milliner's wife. We had a brief conversation, but I told her I had to find Abel before the next dance. I went around the corner to the alley, intending to cut through it to the front of the town hall, but I found Abel with his back to me, ordering Chad to walk to his rented carriage." Jackie paused as Mother Marta stepped up closer to the table.

Sister Francesca handed Jackie a glass of water and she drank some. "Thank you, Sister." Jackie went on relaying what she'd witnessed. "Abel had one of those small derringer guns shoved in Chad's back. It was dark in the alley, and I didn't realize he had a gun in his back until later. All I know is Chad wasn't having any part of it and turned around on him. I heard Abel say something like don't make me do this, and the next thing I knew, he shot Chad in the chest with the derringer. That's when I had a good look at the gun. It was one of those double-barreled pocket-pistol derringers."

"You mean a Remington Model 95, like this?" Arthur pulled a pistol out from behind his back, tucked under his suit coat into the back of his pants.

Jackie's eyes grew wide as she nodded, staring at the pistol. "Only it didn't have a pearl handle like yours. It had walnut or rosewood, perhaps."

Arthur nodded and returned the pistol to his hiding place. "Yep. Remington makes those, too. They're all the same model."

"I guess the sound of the gunshot was muffled by the music, because no one came running after the shot was fired. When I tried to run back to the courtyard for help, everyone had left when I needed them most. There wasn't anyone left outside to help me. They were all inside dancing, where I should have stayed."

Jackie burst into tears and buried her face in her hands. She gathered her composure once again a few seconds later and looked up. Sister Agnes, hard of hearing, moved closer to the table to hear the account better. Jackie seemed strengthened by Agnes moving nearby and continued. "Abel heard me running away and left Chad in the alley to die alone. He followed me to the courtyard and caught up with me before I could make it inside the town hall. I tried to scream, but he covered my face with his hand. He dragged me around to the other side of the building. There, he told me he'd take me home and he'd explain everything on the way if I'd stop crying and screaming. He called it carrying on. On the way home, he threatened me, telling me if I told anyone about what I'd seen, he'd have to kill me, too."

"Did he also explain why he shot Chad at this point; I mean on the drive home?" Hugh inquired, moving away from the kitchen window, stepping closer to them.

Jackie nodded, swiping more tears from her eyes, now red and puffy from crying so much. "He said he hadn't meant to shoot Chad, but since he wouldn't cooperate, he didn't have a choice. He also mentioned something about it all being his brother Cadence's idea. Abel does whatever Cadence wants. They want to buy this town. He kept saying something about when he scared the colonel's grandson away by making it look like Jake killed or kidnapped Chad to win the mayor's election, then they could buy up the rest of the town plots dirt cheap from Jake, and then they'd own Honey River Canyon. Abel told me he'd only planned to kidnap Chad and hold him somewhere in the mountains until people figured he was dead, assuming Jake had done away with him. I guess he planned to abandon me at the dance while he drove Chad up to the mountains, but Chad is a fighter, the son of a cattle rancher. He would never have let a derringer or someone like Abel scare him. He only had respect for shotguns and rifles."

"Do you know where Abel and Cadence are now?" Arthur asked.

"Speaking of Cadence, and his wife, Florence, I don't remember seeing them at the dance when we left, or outside when we found Chad," Josie commented. "They must have slipped away and walked to the hotel."

Jackie nodded toward her sister. "Yes, I believe it was their intention to walk to the hotel at some point after the dance. They were not in the carriage with us when Abel drove me home, and their hired driver must have been dismissed." She turned to Mr. Penworth to answer his question. "I do know they have built a shanty somewhere on Honey River to continue prospecting for gold. I don't know where exactly, but I suspect it is close to Cherry Crossing because Abel has no problem riding to our farm at night. He stays hidden under the cover of darkness among some trees on the back side of our property. I can see him out there, holding up his lantern sometimes. It's like he wants me to know he's there to frighten me into continuing my silence. He is reminding me he can easily harm us, like what he did to Chad."

Jackie paused to drink more of the water. "They still have a suite of rooms at the hotel where Cadence's wife, Florence, stays. She doesn't like to pan for gold with them. They don't need more, but they seem to have an insatiable thirst for it, and now power, too." Jackie sighed. "And I trusted all three of them. I thought they were new friends who could be trusted. I was so wrong. It was killing me inside to know they were trying to destroy Jake, the nice man my sister now loves, and take over our town, and not to mention what they've done to the Martin family; stealing their son's life. Charlie is devastated. Chad is gone. They have lost him forever, and we have lost him forever, or at least until we all go to heaven. And now we might lose Jake, too. For something he didn't even do."

Josie didn't dare look at Jake just then, but she could feel him looking at her, studying her after Jackie had made the remark about Abel destroying the man she loves. Jackie's sobs distracted her, and she turned to look at her sister.

"Between Chad's home-going, and hearing Josie try to sing today, but seeing her burst into tears from grief and frustration about what this is doing to Jake, and reading the newspaper with the false rumors, and living in fear for my life everyday... I had to risk telling the truth for all of us. But I won't lie. I'm scared. Abel and Cadence Keller are two of the most dangerous men I've ever known." Jackie finished relaying all she'd seen, collapsing on Josie's shoulder.

Josie put both of her arms around her. "It's all right, Jackie. You did the right thing coming to us. I'm so proud of you. Everything is going to work out somehow. You'll see."

Chapter Twenty-Four

Be on your guard; stand firm in the faith; be courageous; be strong.

1 Corinthians 16:13, NIV

Jake raked a hand through his hair. "One thing is clear, Jocelyn. You and your sisters aren't safe. You can't return to Cherry Crossing until we put these men behind bars, and the three of you should avoid going anywhere alone until then."

"Yes, but where will we stay?" Josie asked. "We can't go to the hotel. I'm sure the men will return there often when they don't want to be at the claim. Jackie is sure they have plenty of gold from a previous expedition. They can afford whatever they like and a long stay at the hotel if desired."

"You can stay at my mansion. We have all of those empty

bedrooms, and with your sisters there too, and all of my staff, it will be entirely proper," Jake insisted.

Before Josie could protest, and not sure she wanted to protest a perfectly good solution, Mother Marta stepped up closer to the table and put her hands on the edge of it, looking around at all of them. "How are we going to have these men arrested without Sheriff Drummond? 'Tis what I'd like to know." Mother Marta shook her head, her lips pursed together into a firm line. She'd remained quiet until then. Josie had almost forgotten she'd joined them.

"What's happened to the sheriff?" Arthur asked as they all looked at the Mother Superior.

Marta sighed before plunging ahead to explain. "Padre Cornelius stopped by his office this afternoon to inform him of Robin and Star's rescue by Jake here." She motioned toward Jake. "He found the sheriff nearly passed out from a severe case of what he thinks is some sort of influenza. He helped Casey walk upstairs to his residence above the jail and instructed him to stay in bed until Rebecca could arrive. Then he drove out to inform Rebecca Brooks of the situation and asked her to look in on him. While Cornelius was in town however, the sheriff deputized him. At present, Cornelius is the only one in Honey River Canyon with the keys to the jail."

"Padre Cornelius is our deputy? There isn't anyone else to help him?" Jake appeared concerned and apprehensive. "I don't think they'll let a priest shoot anyone, but I guess I'm forgetting this is Montana Territory in the Wild West."

"No, there isn't anyone else unless Sheriff Drummond recovers in time to help us or deputize someone else to help under the circumstances. Cornelius doesn't carry a gun, and I don't think he's ever had to shoot at anyone. He's the son of an Irish sheep farmer. His one exception to shooting has only ever extended to hunting for turkeys, venison, and other wild game to stock the mission smokehouse so we won't starve for lack of meat. The problem is, it's Bishop Thomas who usually returns from these hunts with the most success. Cornelius has far better luck fishing, but he did bring a turkey back one year. Thomas has almost singlehandedly stocked our smokehouse with his excellent hunting skill over the years, but none of you heard this from me. Understand?"

"We won't say anything, Mother Marta," Josie promised, the others nodding.

"This is serious indeed," Sister Francesca agreed. "I have my doubts about Padre Cornelius being able to go after these men with any degree of success. He's more likely to be shot than to lock anyone up."

Sister Agnes put her hands on her hips. "Sisters, where is your faith? Padre Cornelius has something those men will never have!" They all turned to stare at her, wondering what she meant until Agnes clarified. "He has the Lord on his side."

"The sister has a mighty fine point there," Hugh conceded with a smile. Josie couldn't help but wonder why Agnes could hear some conversations so well, like this one. Maybe the Lord had opened her hearing for such a time as this. Her faith seemed contagious. Not one of them hid a smile.

"The good Lord could make it a whole lot easier if he'd just heal our sheriff Casey Drummond," Arthur pointed out. "He'd have these men in jail before sundown."

Sister Francesca sighed. "What are we going to do? We can't

just let these men get away with this. The sheriff could be sick for days or weeks."

Sister Agnes tilted her head to one side. "I think we should have an Esther-Haman dinner."

"What's an Esther-Haman dinner?" Hugh asked, puzzled.

"Like the banquet Esther prepared for the King. She invited Haman, the evildoer, too. Shortly after, the King had him hung. We'll make him a banquet, invite him to join us for dinner at our mission, make him think he and his brother have won some kind of an award or high honor, and then we'll tie him up and throw him in the jail." Agnes smiled as she clenched her hand into a fist as if demonstrating how to catch a pesky fly. "Easy as pie."

"Then all we have to do is wait for the sheriff to recover and the circuit judge to come around." Mother Marta agreed. "I like it."

"I have to admit, the plan sounds easy to execute under the circumstances. We just have to think of some kind of honor to bestow upon him and his brother." Jake's brows furrowed as he appeared to ponder the plan. "Let's work on the details after we all have a good meal and some rest. Miss Josie and Miss Jackie, it's time to head home. We'll get you and your sisters settled into guest rooms at the mansion. I'll send some stable hands out to the cabin to get anything you ladies need."

Jackie turned to her sister. "Don't you dare argue with Jake. This man loves you, Josie. It's the most obvious thing I've ever seen. He'll protect us. We need the safety of numbers and being in town with your strong man and his nice friend, where Abel and his brother can't hurt us."

Josie chose not to respond to her sister. She'd mentioned

love too many times in front of far too many people. "Thank you, Jake. My sisters and I will be happy and thankful to accept your offer of protection, but this doesn't have anything to do with us. There's still the matter of my horse standing between us and love. I'll be outside on Mrs. Velvet, ready to follow Jillian and Jacqueline in the wagon. I'm cold, hungry, and tired. Let's get home, I mean, to the mansion, quickly." She tilted her chin and marched out of the kitchen as Sister Francesca inspected the timepiece pinned to her habit. Josie didn't need Jacqueline to frighten Jake with such talk. She could hear Sister Francesca herding the rest of them to follow behind her.

"Yes, time to feed these children their supper, and then prayers, and then tuck them in bed. You must all hurry on home now. It's much later than I thought." Sister Francesca herded them toward the dining hall to follow Josie. "Good night, everyone. 'Tis been a long day. We all need a good meal and then sleep."

Chapter Twenty-Five

Blessed is the one who perseveres under trial because, having stood the test, that person will receive the crown of life that the Lord has promised to those who love Him.

James 1:12, NIV

The mission quickly emptied of all their guests, waving good-bye to Mother Marta as she stood at the door. Ellie had departed some time ago, or the party would have offered her a ride home despite the fact she lived in the opposite direction of town.

Josie reached her horse, tethered beside Jillian and their wagon. She stepped into the stirrup and swung up into the saddle, spreading her skirts about so she wouldn't look too unladylike since she'd had enough with riding side saddle lately.

"We're all heading to the mayor's mansion," she informed Jill. "Here comes Jackie. She can ride with you and fill you in on all the details."

"All right," sweet Jillian nodded. She hardly ever gave Josie a problem, but at the moment, Josie could have strangled Jackie. *Lord help me to forgive Jackie's words about the state of our hearts, and please help keep us safe. Help us capture these evil men.*

"Jake says it's not safe to return home until Abel is behind bars, and maybe his brother, too." Jackie climbed into the wagon with Jill. "I suppose you've heard we're going to stay at the mayor's mansion for a while."

"I have," Jillian replied. "I'm anxious to hear about the long discussion in the kitchen. I could see everyone talking through the windows. No sign of Abel though, but we're ready. I've got the shotgun under the seat."

Jackie straightened her skirts. "Good, but I'm feeling much safer with these capable men around us. They'll escort us, and I'll tell you all about the rest as we drive."

Josie leaned toward her sisters from her mount. "No more talk about the matters of heart between Jake and me. You'll only add tension to our new and fragile relationship."

"I'm sorry, Josie. It's just so obvious you two are meant for each other," Jackie insisted.

"Hush, here they come," Josie hissed.

"I promise to say no more." Her middle sister smiled and sat back in the seat.

Josie waited until the men were settled on their mounts. Then she steered Mrs. Velvet to ride alongside Jake as they followed the wagon, which followed Hugh and Arthur. They rode in silence all the way into town, trying to process all her sister had shared.

When they reached the mayor's mansion and the stable behind it, Josie sighed with relief as several servants sprang into action to tend to the horses while Jake led them all inside the side door. There, Mrs. Maddie Penworth greeted them.

"The Hayes sisters will be our honored guests for a while, Mrs. Penworth. If you could add three place settings to the dinner table and show the ladies to our best guest rooms. I'd like Josie to have my mother's room, and her sisters, some rooms close by. Anything they require, if you could please see their needs are met. Also, from here on, we need to be certain the doors and windows are kept locked for safety reasons. When the ladies provide us with a list, we'll send someone at once to Cherry Crossing to retrieve the items, and once daily to care for their livestock."

Jake looked at Josie as if to see if his instructions met with her approval. Josie curtsied slightly. "Thank you for your generosity and kindness, Mr. Hunter. It means a great deal to us."

"Very good then," Jake said. "You are in good hands with our housekeeper. She is the very best."

"Would you like dinner served in half an hour, sir?" Maddie asked.

"Yes, a half an hour will be fine," Jake agreed.

"Right this way, ladies." Mrs. Penworth smiled at Josie and her sisters. "How nice for the house to have company. It's starting to feel more like when Colonel Bradshaw was with us, God rest his soul."

Mrs. Penworth led them to their rooms, and Josie thought

she'd nearly died and gone to heaven at the sight of the bed alone in her guest quarters. The canopy bed boasted fine quality linens, feather pillows, and brocade curtains around it. These could be closed to keep warm at night.

Maddie fluffed a few pillows on the bed as Josie and her sisters looked around. "This was Jake's mother's room. We have had few guests given the honor of using it. If it meets with your satisfaction, I'll return in about ten minutes for your list of items you'll need from your home after I show your sisters to their rooms."

"Certainly, yes, I'll have a list ready. This room is beautiful and thank you..." Josie wondered if she could perhaps be in a dream. The housekeeper nodded and led her sisters down the hall, chatting as she went, her voice drifting into Josie's open door.

Josie continued to look around, hardly able to touch anything. Everything looked so exquisitely beautiful. She had her own sitting area by the fireplace with a chaise lounge and several armchairs for reading. Dark cherrywood furniture filled the room, including a bureau with a tall mirror, a vanity, an oval full-length mirror on its own stand, a writing desk, and a wardrobe. Two recessed window seats faced the stable and gardens in the rear, creating more lovely locations for reading. The room's color palette included everything in shades of magenta rose, pale soft pinks, and cream.

She glanced in the mirror at her dark tresses, wondering what she could possibly wear to dinner other than the black dress she still wore in honor of Chad's home-going, but when Maddie returned for the list of items she wanted from home, she reminded her to make use of anything in the wardrobe until then. "I'll also send up one of the maids to style your hair, ma'am."

"Thank you." Josie nodded, handing her the list she'd made at the writing desk.

Her sisters returned to her room after giving Maddie their lists, both chatting about their elegant, luxurious rooms. "What do you think of this dress, Jocelyn?" Jackie held a pastel blue chiffon evening gown up to her shoulders and swirled around with it. "The housekeeper said we could wear anything in the wardrobes."

"I found this violet dress with a bustle in my wardrobe, Josie. What will you wear?" Jillian asked.

"I don't know. I'm not sure if I should rummage through someone else's clothing." Josie sighed. "I'm not sure I should remove these mourning clothes, either."

"Of course, you should!" Jackie tossed the blue dress onto Josie's bed and crossed the room to rummage through the wardrobe. Jill came to her side to assist. "Maybe this one? Look at the lovely rosettes on the right shoulder."

"No, I think this one. It's understated and fits Josie's personality more," Jillian said, drawing a forest green evening gown from the wardrobe. "It has the chiffon overlay, no rosettes, no silk, three-quarter length sleeves, the wrapping pigeon-front bodice, and it flows out from the waistband to the floor. The layers of skirting move so nicely together. No bustle. Josie would look perfect in this."

"I do believe you are right," Jackie concurred. "What do you think, Josie? If you don't wear one, we can't wear ours. It won't look right. Either we all dress for dinner, or none of us."

Josie surveyed the gown with some hesitation. "It is pretty. I suppose it couldn't hurt, but are you girls sure? At some point, we'll have to return home to our worn calico dresses and old work aprons."

Jackie nodded. "We are sure. These beautiful gowns are just wasting away, waiting for pretty ladies to make good use of them. I knew Estelle had hosted fine parties at the mansion before, but I had no idea she kept some of the latest styles on hand in case someone needed to borrow something. Let us have a few days of enjoyment after all the suffering we've been through of late."

Josie sighed, relenting. "All right, but we must help each other with our hair and getting dressed until the maid makes the rounds. We can't make the gentlemen wait on us by being late to dinner. It's considered rude. We must hurry."

When the girls came downstairs twenty minutes later, Jake and Hugh, exiting the library, heard them talking as they descended the staircase. Hugh looked up and whistled, and Jake grinned, his eyes only on Josie. "Ladies, you look so beautiful, as always," Jake said, extending an arm for Josie. Hugh held out his arms to escort both of her sisters to the formal dining room.

"Thank you, Jake." Josie smiled at him, deeply appreciative of his concern and protection for them. The very idea of someone lurking around at Cherry Crossing in the night hours bothered her. "Everything is exceptionally nice. We truly appreciate what you're doing for us. My sisters and I are elated."

"Good," Jake replied as he led them down the main hall. "I'm glad to be of help. I hope you like rosemary chicken with cornbread stuffing, new potatoes, and baby carrots."

"We do," she smiled as Jake turned at the first corner of the hall. "It smells delicious."

"I hear dessert is a chocolate raspberry cake with a vanilla glazed icing," Hugh commented from behind them, "but wait until you try the French mushrooms on toast and the chutney. There will be a salad of spring greens offered, too."

"It sounds divine," Josie replied over the wonder and merriment of her sisters as they entered the dining room.

Jake pulled out a seat to his right for Josie, and Hugh pulled out seats for her sisters. Josie couldn't imagine what they'd have done without Hugh's presence to help keep things balanced by giving his attention to her sisters. She knew she would feel sad when he had to leave Honey River Canyon.

Jake prayed, blessing the food, and asking for the Lord's continued protection. Then he removed the warming lid covering his plate. Josie and her sisters observed his actions and did the same as a servant came behind each of them and removed the lids from the table.

"We'll all sleep better for the first time since the dance." Hugh spooned some of the chutney onto his chicken, and then reached for several slices of the mushroom toast offered by Tolliver on an appetizer tray.

"Definitely. I know the Lord answered a lot of our prayers today, in great part thanks to Miss Jacqueline's courage to come forward." Jake nodded in her direction, and Jackie smiled back at him, basking in his praise.

"I know I will sleep better knowing we are safer here with you than at the cabin with a murderer lurking about on our property." Jackie sliced into some of her chicken.

"What are we to do while we are here?" Jill asked her sisters. "Should we help the nuns prepare the feast?"

"Please, ladies, use the library, play the piano, walk in our

188

gardens, make yourselves at home," Jake insisted. "Enjoy being closer to town and peruse the shops, or feel welcome to visit the mission, but do be careful not to do anything alone. Please ask Arthur or Maddie to arrange for a member of our staff to accompany you. There is safety in numbers."

Josie agreed, finding Jake's hospitality a blessing as she considered the alternative. What if Abel Keller had attempted to harm her sister, or any of them. He'd already proven his capabilities. "I agree with you. The more I think about what could have happened over the past few days, the happier I am you have opened your home and resources to us."

"I think I'll send a telegram to my fiancée tomorrow. I can't think about returning to Philadelphia until Abel, and maybe his brother, are behind bars." Hugh tasted some of the rosemary chicken on his plate. "This is so delicious. I wish we had your cook back home."

"Sally Danvers is an excellent cook," Jake agreed. He tasted some of the mushroom toast. "I'm not sure we can technically put Abel's brother behind bars unless we have more evidence."

Hugh's brows furrowed. "We have Ellie's testimony. Remember, she said she heard the other man step up to his side and called him Abel when he told him to hurry up and have the note delivered. I think 'tis enough evidence when combined with Miss Jacqueline's testimony about him doing his brother's bidding. I also think Abel will take his brother down with him. He may testify his brother masterminded the scheme."

Jake paused to consider Hugh's points as he added some pepper to another slice of the mushroom toast. "All good reasons to lock both up then. Tomorrow, we must ride out to the mission after breakfast and tell the nuns to invite both brothers to their feast."

"I'll go with you," Josie said. "I need to keep my hands busy until they are captured."

Jill and Jackie exchanged a look and nodded between themselves before Jill spoke up. "We'll go with you, too."

"Yes, I can be ready to accompany you, as well. I can send the telegram the day after tomorrow or the next day maybe. On second thought, this whole thing might be over then, and I can return to Philadelphia soon." Hugh sliced into more of his chicken.

Jake nodded. "'Tis settled then. We'll all ride out to the mission after breakfast. Maybe a good reason to use my grandfather's coach. I've been wanting to try it out, and although the carriage might be cooler with the weather warming up, I think the coach might be safer. I won't feel like we are prairie dogs popping up as targets when we reach the plains area near the mission."

"The coach sounds fine with me," Hugh commented.

After the meal, Jake offered to show them the library, where they each selected books to read, disappearing from the room with yawns and various excuses after the long day. Josie could have perused those floor-to-ceiling shelves for hours if it hadn't turned into such an eventful day with Chad's home-going in the morning and her sister's revelation at the mission.

Finding herself alone with her benefactor, a man who could make her knees tremble from only one kiss, she didn't want to remain there alone with him. Not only because of impropriety, but more because she had to acknowledge one fact. She didn't trust her desires if left alone with him for too long in such a romantic setting with books, candles, fine leather armchairs she could sit in for an entire day, and a gentleman as attractive as Jacob Hunter. Deciding it best to follow her sisters while she could still hear their footsteps climbing the steps, and weary from the day's events, Josie tucked a copy of *North and South* by Elizabeth Gaskell under her arm. She headed for the door to exit the library. Turning at the door, she paused. "Good night, Jake. Thank you again for all you are doing for us. I hope your name will be completely cleared soon."

"Thank you," he said, bowing slightly, his golden-blond hair glowing in the candlelight and oil lamps placed around the room.

Josie and her sisters arrived at breakfast at eight o'clock in the morning, ready to face the day. Their items delivered from the cabin had made dressing so much easier. She had her writing papers and journals, her Bible to continue with her daily devotional time, and her own clothing and toiletry items. Her sisters seemed happy to have their personal items at their disposal, as well.

Hugh and Jake looked completely absorbed as they each read their own copies of the newspaper while she and her sisters filled their plates with items on the buffet in the dining room. Josie selected some scrambled eggs, a medley of fruit, and a warm, flaky biscuit. At the table, she poured herself a cup of coffee and added some cream from the pitcher, drinking a few sips before she looked up to see the men could barely contain gleeful looks on their faces.

"This is fantastic, Jake. You're a hero!" Hugh passed his newspaper across the table to Josie. "Have a look at this, Miss Jocelyn."

Josie reached for the paper. It read, *Honey River Gazette Special Edition*, across the top. The headline to the main featured story read, "Jake Hunter Rescues Orphans." Josie smiled as she read the article, happy to see him spoken of in a manner worthy of his character. Townsfolk would no longer find it easy to believe him capable of cold-blooded murder.

"Tell the truth, Josie. Did you say something to the folks who own the newspaper?" Jake asked. "The article barely mentions you, and yet you did most of the hard work finding them."

"No, I didn't say a word. I have no idea who did, but perhaps someone from the mission," she replied. "I don't have a problem with any of this story. You're the one who pulled Robin and Star up from the ledge, and I wouldn't have had any rope if you hadn't arrived."

"May I read it?" Jill asked as she joined them at the table.

Josie handed her the copy she'd finished reading, but like Jake, she couldn't help but wonder who had shared the story with Sheldon and Twila Thornton. Perhaps it would remain a mystery, but she sure would like to offer her gratitude. She bowed her head and gave silent thanks for the meal, the safety of her family, her lavish surroundings, and the unraveling of the mystery concerning Chad Martin's passing. *Please Lord, bring swift justice and clear Jake's name. Make Honey River Canyon and Cherry Crossing safe again.*

Chapter Twenty-Six

Be strong and take heart, all you who hope in the Lord.

Psalm 31:24, NIV

Sister Agnes hid behind a female mannequin wearing a fringed cowgirl dress near the front doors where they'd followed the Keller individual inside. She didn't mind the fringed cowgirl dress, but she couldn't help but wonder if the shotgun the mannequin posed with happened to be loaded with real ammunition or not. The mannequin stood beside a sign tacked to the community bulletin wall of Bradshaw's Trading Post. Sister Angel stood just inches from it, attempting to read the sign, squinting through her broken spectacles to see the words, *Bull Riding & Trick Pony Rider Wild West Show.*

Sister Angel smiled, forgetting about the errand they'd set

out to accomplish for the moment. "Sister Agnes, it says here this Wild West show is coming to Honey River Canyon in June. I think our children would love to see something like this. Admission is ten cents each for children, and twenty-five cents each for adults. Inflation is killing this country! Can you believe these prices, Sister?"

Sister Agnes hadn't heard much of whatever Sister Angel had said. Number one, she'd read the sign on the way in, and if it's what she muttered about, she'd already decided on attending the western show, but her hearing had chosen to abandon her, at least for the moment. Number two, directly behind the mannequin, she'd spotted a shelf with Daniel Boone styled coonskin hats, and she'd always wanted one. Her wrinkled hands trembled as she ruffled through the shelf, searching for one to try on. They really should get away from the mission and come to town more often, if only her aging body would cooperate. She found the hat she liked, realizing they all looked about the same, most sized about the same, too. She pulled it on over the veil and coif of her habit, the fur tickling the skin on her cheek. She ran her hand over the tail and the silky fur made her giggle like a schoolgirl.

"Sister!" she called out in her scratchy voice. "How do I look, Sister?" Turning to her right, she nearly jumped a mile. Sister Angel stood right beside her with her hands on her hips, tapping one foot as if she'd committed a cardinal sin.

"Oh, Sister Angel! I didn't see you standing there. How do you like my hat?" She grinned and reached up to touch the fur again. It felt so soft. The children would love her hat.

"Sister Agnes, he's gotten away. We're supposed to deliver the invitation like Jake and Mother Marta asked, remember?

Not shop for silly coonskin hats we'll never wear." Sister Angel looked positively aggravated.

"Did you say deliver the indignation? Oh yes, the invitation." Sister Agnes promptly removed the hat and flung it onto the shelving. Miraculously, it landed on the right shelf, almost exactly where she'd found it. She turned to Sister Angel and pointed at the man they'd identified earlier at the General Store as Abel Keller, thanks to a little help from Katy Emmerson. "Sister Angel, you're letting him get away! Hurry!"

Sister Angel threw her hands up in the air. She took Agnes by the hand, and they hurried out of the trading post to their buggy, tied to the hitching post in front. By the time they'd both managed to climb inside it however, Abel Keller had managed to walk halfway to the hotel.

"Can't you drive any faster?" Sister Agnes asked, horrified Abel might escape. "We dare not lose him. The Lord is counting on us to help Him administer justice, Sister."

"I'm trying, Sister Agnes, but I have to be careful not to run anyone over. I've only got one eye working until my new eyeglasses arrive, you know." Sister Angel looked to her right and then her left. "Is the coast clear?"

"All clear," Agnes replied.

"Yaw!" Sister Angel snapped the reins gently but firmly, and the horse shot into a gallop. "Hold on, Sister!"

"I'm holding on!" Agnes hollered back, clasping a hand to anything she could find. Soon, they'd caught up with Abel and she waved at him, hoping to catch his attention. She stopped waving long enough to make the sign of the cross over herself and sent a prayer to the Lord for the success of their mission. How she loved serving Jesus; the adventures and wonders never ceased. "Oh, Angel, you are such a reckless driver. Are we going to be arrested for speeding?" Her eyes danced with excitement. She laughed as they continued, passing Abel.

"The Sheriff is sick, remember?" Angel chuckled. "With our deputy, we have favor, sister. Great favor, but he's busy conducting morning prayers at the mission. Hang on tight. I need to make this fancy left turn to block the target."

Abel Keller glanced over his shoulder at the buggy with the nuns driving it. He'd seen them at Emmerson's General Store where he'd purchased a new pair of work gloves, and again at Bradshaw's Trading Post on the corner of the town square near the mayor's mansion. The trading post happened to sell the only gold-panning sieves in town, and his had broken. *No, surely, they were not following him, were they?* He tried to hurry his pace along. If he could make it to the hotel, he could escape their scrutiny.

As he considered the nuns, quickening his pace on the boardwalk, he figured they probably wanted to ask him to attend church. He'd heard about their mission, but a Catholic he was not. In fact, he didn't usually attend any church of any particular denomination except for here and there. *Oh, good heavens!* They were following him, waving at him in fact, trying to catch up with him as they barreled down the street with their habit black veils flying out behind them. Perhaps he should run before they cornered him. Another glance, and he saw them gaining speed on his position. He should indeed run for his life unless he desired to become Catholic, which he did not.

To his utter dismay, he could see the nun in his peripheral vision begin to pass him and then yank the reins a hard right, causing the horse to turn the buggy left into the alley immediately before the hotel, effectively blocking him from proceeding. The nun pulled the reins toward herself, yelling, "Whoa! Whoa boy!"

She impressed him with her expert steering skills as the horse stopped the buggy in the alley in front of him, and the two nuns weathered the sudden stop without too much trouble, but one of them kept making the sign of the cross over herself. He'd have had a case of whiplash, but they seemed accustomed to the erratic driving. He supposed they could get away with a great deal of unlawful things out here in the Wild West, as he and his brother had done themselves time and time again. He pushed the thoughts from his mind as the nun holding the reins yelled, "Abel Keller, stop right there!"

Her very words arrested his progress. He couldn't take another step. She sounded like his mother, for one thing. For another, she knew his name, which meant there might be no end in sight to future expeditions to contact him to invite him to church. He had best stop and hear what she had to say.

Before he could address them with any words of greeting, however, the nun in the passenger seat reached in a pocket of her long black habit and handed the other nun a sealed note, who immediately held the note out toward him. "An invitation, sir."

"And not just any invitation, we should add," the passenger nun said with a smile lighting up her eyes.

"Sister Agnes is right. This is a very special invitation, sir.

It's our pleasure to finally meet you in person. We've heard so much about you. I'm Sister Angel, by the way."

"A *special* invitation?" Abel repeated, his brow rising as he stared at the note as if it contained a disease inside. Dare he accept it? If he reached out and touched it, and actually accepted it, he might be bound to it. Then again, what could they mean by a special invitation? Would he be given a special dignified box to sit in with his family at the church service, or was it only the Lutherans and Presbyterians who had family pew boxes? He couldn't recall exactly, nor could he grasp what on earth they meant. Perhaps they required a sizeable donation of some sort to have such a pew.

"What sort of special invitation do you mean, exactly?" His mouth twisted to one side, skeptical of anything they might have to say.

"Padre Cornelius and the Mother Superior wish to invite you and your family to dinner this evening as our honored guests," Sister Agnes explained, leaning forward to peer at him over Sister Angel's shoulder. "They've heard about your work."

"Dinner this evening?" he repeated. "They've heard about my work?" He didn't know this padre or this superior mother, but they sounded important.

The nun nodded. "To honor the wonderful work you are doing, sir. Yes, the dinner is this evening at the St. Paul Mission on Bell Avenue at seven-thirty. We're on the far southwest edge of town out in the countryside a bit. You can't miss it. We have an L-shaped building, and it has a bell tower above the chapel and nave." Sister Angel urged him to take the note once more, and he reluctantly reached up and accepted it, exasperated.

Opening it, he read the handwritten invitation signed by Padre Cornelius.

"Once word gets out about the gold prospecting you're doing, this town will boom, and we'll have you and your brother to thank for our prosperity." Sister Angel smiled at him approvingly.

"Yes, indeed. This town will consider you a real trail blazer," Sister Agnes said. "I admire trail blazing in a man such as your-self and your brother."

This constituted the first thing they'd said making any sense to him. He sputtered in surprise. "W-well now, how nice of you to think of us in a manner befitting the kind of work we do. Seven-thirty, you say?"

"Seven-thirty sharp. And we'll have plenty of food. Ante-lope, buffalo, venison steak, lemon chicken, huckleberry peach pie, apple pie, blackberry cobbler, stewed tomatoes with our homemade corn relish, parsley new potatoes, oyster stuffing, carrot raisin salad, lima beans, creamed peas with pearl onions, and my personal favorite, potatoes julienne ..." Sister Agnes leaned forward and breathed in the air as if already smelling the divine list of dishes she'd mentioned. "You should know the sweet Hayes girl we heard you escorted to the dance will be there with her sisters, and of course, a few others in our town who respect and admire what you're accomplishing for us. We're all rooting for your continued success in finding gold."

"And we will have some entertainment after dinner. Bishop Thomas has offered to do a reading from Charles Dickens, and the children are putting together a surprise entirely in your honor," Sister Angel said.

"I certainly can see you have gone to a great deal of effort in our honor. It is rather short notice, and I'm not sure if Cade and Florence can be in attendance, but I will do my best to persuade them. In any case, I will most certainly attend, sisters." Abel smiled at them. "I guess it'd be fair to say we need all the prayers we can get in our line of work, and of course, for the ultimate good of the town."

"You can say that again," Agnes muttered under her breath with a cough.

"Pardon?" he asked.

Sister Agnes coughed again and cleared her throat. "I was just saying you're mighty high on my prayer list. I do hope this cough won't prevent me from enjoying the evening."

"We should be going and fix you another cup of broth, sister." Angel looked over at Abel. "Please do extend our apologies for the lateness of our invitation. We tried to deliver it yesterday, but..." Sister Angel faltered.

Agnes interrupted her. "I'm afraid I'm to blame for the delay. My achy bones were acting up again. 'Tis entirely my fault. Sister Angel had to stay put at the mission the past few days and help cover for my absence while I stayed in bed instead of helping like I should. Thanks to some good old-fashioned chicken broth, hot tea, and plenty of rest, I'm good as new today. Hence we are out and about, running our errands. Well, almost new. Except for a few wrinkles ..." Agnes chuckled at herself, and he and Sister Angel joined in before they said farewell and waved good-bye. "See you tonight, Mr. Keller!"

Abel drew in a sigh of relief as he held up the invitation and smiled. At least they could finally be included to an exclusive dinner with a few of the right people in town. His brother only wanted to know the right sort of people, and these nuns and their connections seemed like the right sort to him. They had to be closer to God than himself, and maybe it would count for something in Heaven's eyes. He had to think about turning a new leaf in this town, and maybe this invitation and these peculiar nuns could spur him onto a better sort of path. If his brother didn't have so many crooked plans involving such unspeakable deeds. He did rather like the Hayes girl, but she had turned up at precisely the wrong moment, and now the whole of how things had turned out depended on if she kept her mouth shut.

Chapter Twenty-Seven

No weapon that is formed against thee shall prosper; and every
tongue that shall rise against thee in judgment thou shalt
condemn. This is the heritage of the servants of the Lord, and
their righteousness is of me, saith the Lord.

Isaiah 54:17

Josie peeked outside the mission's kitchen window to see a rented carriage arrive from the livery bearing Abel, Cadence, and Florence Keller. "Places everyone! They are here. All three of them." Josie lingered at the window where she could observe as everyone scrambled into position. Some dove into hiding, and others would remain out in the open, but no matter the assigned place, the plan required some degree of composure in execution. It also required the Lord's blessing. Josie, her sisters, Jake, Hugh, and many others now involved, along with those at the mission, had spent some time during the afternoon hours in the chapel on their knees, praying, believing, and hoping for a good outcome.

Padre Cornelius and Mother Marta proceeded to the mission entrance to welcome their guests, stepping outside at the right moment looking poised, calm, and assured. So far so good, Josie decided, but she reminded herself the evening had barely begun as she took her seat in the dining hall. The nuns had spent much of the day cooking the elaborate feast. Everything smelled and looked delicious. Platters, bowls, and other dishes of food filled the tables. A fire in the fireplace cast a bright glow around the dining hall, and candles, lanterns, and sconces flickered their lights. Each table had several vases of late spring blooms, picked by some of the children, dotting the tables. The older female students had set the plates, silverware, and linen napkins at each place setting. Then they'd made place cards with each guest's name, designating where each person would sit, since this vital part of the plan would contribute to their success in capturing the Keller men.

Padre Cornelius escorted the guests into the hall, introducing the Mother Superior, Bishop Thomas, and then the other nuns after he led them to their seats. Everyone stood behind their chairs, the benches replaced with chairs for all adults except at the children's table. On this day, the male and female students would sit together at one table, adults at the other two. He motioned toward the children, and introduced the Hayes sisters, Jake, Hugh, and some important individuals from the community they had invited to help the Keller brothers feel honored. These included Maxheimer and Grace Lewis, the flour mill owners; Henry and Cora Fields, the town bankers; and Lila and Jared Hopkins, the only large dairy farmers in the region. Hiding in the kitchen, Joshua and Charlie Martin remained out of sight with their shotguns, positioned in the pantry with the curtain pulled shut. Josie could only hope and pray they wouldn't try to take things too far in seeking revenge. To this point, they seemed cohesive to follow the plan.

"Please, be seated everyone. I will say grace." Chairs scraped on the stone floors as they sat down, and then Father Cornelius said a blessing over the meal. He spoke a few words to thank their guests of honor, explaining how townsfolk held their efforts in high regard, and he reiterated the hope resting in their work to create what they believed would turn Honey River Canyon into a boom town. "A toast, to our new friends and honored guests, the Keller brothers, Cadence and Abel."

Sister Angel offered to pour Spanish imported wine from Madrid, a gift to the mission, into Cade and Abel's challis cups. "'Tis our very best bottle, to celebrate your continued success."

Cade nodded, and Abel held out his challis with his brother. He smiled. "Thank you, Sister Angel."

Angel filled their cups to the brim and placed the remains of the wine nearby so they could refill them liberally. This idea from Mother Marta could save lives if the Keller brothers became subdued enough to let their guard down.

The meal progressed with some polite talk about the weather, farming issues, and other pleasantries. Abel seemed happy to find himself seated beside his brother and wife, but also across from Jackie, Mother Marta, and the Fields. Josie observed everything in silence, thankful Jake sat on her right. His presence reassured her for some reason, and she chalked it up to the fact he and Hugh had firearms. In fact, they sat in seats where they could produce their pistols and aim directly at the Keller brothers at precisely the right time.

Before anyone finished half of their meal, Padre Cornelius invited one of the older students, Rachel, to read a few lines from a poem by Alfred Tennyson. Everyone clapped. She sat down, and Josie prayed for the next part of the plan. They'd had such little time to prepare, and a great number of individuals now knew the truth, but if any among them acted oddly, the plan could backfire and fail.

Padre smiled. "Well done, Rachel. And now, before a Dickens reading by my esteemed colleague and friend, Bishop Thomas, we have some roping tricks, as presented by a talented local boy, Samuel." Father Cornelius sat down, and Samuel took his place in the center of the room, twirling his lasso until it went up higher and higher. Josie had taken a guess the Keller brothers didn't know Samuel as Chad's youngest sibling. They hadn't attended the funeral, and if they'd read the obituary, it hadn't mentioned much about him. Samuel could rope just about anything. He could do all sorts of roping tricks and maneuvers.

His lasso mesmerized them all as he completed several fancy rope tricks to his right and left. Everyone clapped after these. He then kept the rope moving upward by swirling the lasso up high. When it was high enough, Samuel took everyone by surprise when he turned, yanking the lasso to his left as it came down around the Keller brothers. He pulled it tight around their arms as the brothers laughed, thinking it all part of the show, especially when everyone clapped. They had no idea folks clapped for Samuel's precision as much as the objects of it.

This, they'd rehearsed and practiced with Samuel, and only after Chad's mother and father had heard the plan and agreed to it. At this moment, as Samuel pulled the lasso tightly around Abel and Cadence and the applause faded, all the other men present, including Jake and Hugh, with previously hidden pistols, took aim on them while Padre Cornelius and Bishop Thomas moved in place to help Samuel hold the rope firm. The Keller brothers began to struggle against the rope, but with guns aimed on them and the Martins entering from the kitchen also pointing shotguns in their direction, they soon realized struggle remained in vain.

"Well done, Samuel. Here Charlie." Joshua Martin tossed more rope to his son. "Tie them up real good."

Padre took charge, surprising Josie when he pulled his temporary deputy badge out and pinned it on his priestly plain brown frock. "Let's get them into the wagon, chairs and all, and lock them up in the jail. Don't cry Florence. At least we aren't locking you behind bars. Trust me when I say there won't be any amount of gold you can post as bail for these two."

The children, guests, and the nuns did not clap again. When Mother Marta stood, they knew to remain silent as her chair scraped against the stone floor in the hall.

"I'll get you for this, Padre," Cadence hollered as Mr. Emmerson, Mr. Fields, and Mr. Lewis hoisted the captives in their chairs up and out of the dining hall, and then into the wagon waiting to take them to jail. When the men reached the main hall however, a clamor erupted as everyone rose to follow, cloistering around the door of the mission to observe the men enforcing the Keller boys to embrace their fate. Florence Keller, however, pursued, pushing her way through the crowd to escape the mission. She ran to the carriage they'd rented, brushing away tears. She climbed inside it, instructing her driver waiting outside the mission to take her to the hotel in town.

Some of the men climbed into the mission's wagon with their prisoners while others surrounded it on horseback in posse fashion, ready to escort the Keller brothers to their fate of a cold jail cell. Padre Cornelius had secured the keys to the jail along with the mission keys he wore onto his rope belt, choosing to ride in the buggy with Bishop Thomas.

"Let's move out, men," Padre said with a forward swing of his arm as Thomas snapped the reins. They followed the rented carriage, the wagon with their prisoners, and others escorting on horseback toward town.

Josie leaned against her sisters, huddling at the door with Mother Marta as she held a lantern in the darkness while they watched the procession disappear onto the road, thankful their nightmare had come to an end. Jake's name would finally be completely restored, Chad and his family would have justice, and peace could return to Honey River Canyon once again, not to be underestimated or taken for granted by its inhabitants.

"Let's go inside, ladies, children. We'll finish our meal in peace, pray for the safety of our men until they return, and for the speedy recovery of our sheriff's health." Mother Marta turned around, herding the ladies and students back inside. "Well done, everyone. Well done. Thank the Lord, not a single shot had to be fired at our mission."

Jackie tucked her arm in Josie's, her face looking somewhat downcast. "As happy as I am about things turning out well, I admit I am terribly sad it means we'll be leaving Jake's mansion. He sends men to tend our farm, and everything is terribly nice there, and oh, the dresses..." Josie felt awkward about residing at the mansion, but she knew it pleased Jake, so she didn't respond. Perhaps they would stay with Jake a little while longer, but she knew it could not last forever.

Chapter Twenty-Eight

I believe in the compelling power of love. I do not understand it. I believe it to be the most fragrant blossom of all this thorny existence.

—Theodore Dreiser, American novelist and journalist

Upon his recovery a few days later, Sheriff Drummond exuded delight with the capture and arrest of his new prisoners, including the story of how it had all transpired. He officially hired Father Cornelius as his deputy, with the understanding the mission came first. They had agreed Padre would only assist in emergency situations and on a few other special occasions as he could, if needed. The circuit judge came around twice a year on a Tuesday, and Josie had a feeling the Keller brothers desperately needed a long imprisonment to consider their repentance.

Padre, however, began taking shooting practice seriously from then on, but Josie decided she'd never adapt to the idea. She still found it a little odd to see Cornelius standing outside behind the mission shooting at stacks of soda water bottles with a pistol. Maybe it was on account of him wearing his customary, long brown priestly garb made of thick wool in all types of weather, his waist tied with a short length of rope, a large metal cross necklace dangling on a strip of leather from around his neck. Nonetheless, he wore his new badge proudly, and he had indeed earned it. Maybe it was on account of the fact she couldn't picture him riding a horse, nor could she picture him chasing a bank robber or gun-slinging troublemaker in one of the mission's buggies or a wagon. In any case, she and her sisters slept better knowing bars kept cunning, evil men away from Cherry Crossing.

Hugh left for Philadelphia in early May, a week later, on the same day Jocelyn and her sisters returned to Cherry Crossing. After his summer wedding to Gwendolyn Smith, he planned to help his father with their country house and various farming duties, as well as seek a position as a clergyman, promising to visit in the future. Josie and her sisters only agreed to stay the extra week at Jake's insistence they should rest and enjoy Hugh's company before his departure. They read books, played parlor games, strolled through the garden, and danced when Josie or Jake took turns playing the piano. On Sunday, they attended church together. However, Josie found herself anxious to return to the cabin so she could have time to write, harvest the hay, check the crops, ride their horses, and tend the kitchen garden. As much as she'd relished her time getting to know Jake and more about Hugh, hearing stories about Philadelphia over scrumptious meals around the mansion's dinner table while dressed in beautiful evening gowns they sometimes borrowed from the guest wardrobes, she knew their visit must come to an end.

Jake took her in his arms and gave her a sweet farewell kiss before her departure, pulling her into a recessed corner of the library, velvet drapes with gold cords hiding them from the world. "I don't want you to go," he said, his strong arms pushing against the wall on either side of her shoulders.

"Nor do I, and yet I must," she replied softly.

"May I court you properly, Miss Jocelyn Hayes?" He moved a stray wisp of hair from her face, tucking it into her other curls. "Miss Josie with the chocolate hair and beautiful molasses eyes?"

"That depends." She glanced at his blue eyes, too shy, alone in his presence, to tell him they were the color of Montana's beautiful great big sky, but she could not hide a coy smile, the result of pure joy at hearing his question.

"And on what does this depend?" he asked, studying her.

"Does your request mean you have intentions, sir?"

He returned a smile. "For a moment there, I thought you'd say something about my horse."

"Well, if you have truly honorable intentions, Blue, shall by virtue of marriage, become our horse, and therefore the argument becomes mute, does it not? As Pa used to tell my mother, what's mine is yours, and what's yours is mine ... so everything is ours."

Pulling her close, Jake smiled, kissing her. "How I love the sound of that ..." Then he nuzzled her ear. "Yes, my belligerent beauty, I have honorable intentions, and I won't want to wait very long to make them known. I know you've held on strong for a long time, but if you'll hold on a little while longer, I'll see to it you never have to work so hard ever again. You may devote your life to writing and pursuits of your choice and preference."

His kiss tickled her ear, causing her to laugh, pushing him away from her ear. When he gazed into her eyes once again, she replied, "Then yes, you may officially court me, properly." She could have thrown her arms around him for all he'd said. *How did he know? Why did it seem like he could see inside her heart and soul at times?*

"And you understand I may again become a man of the cloth since our town only has a circuit preacher," he said.

"I certainly hope so," Josie replied. "It's one of the things I love best about you, Jake Hunter."

He smiled in response, and she permitted him one last kiss before her departure for home, hoping she would not find the coming months too long before they could be together always.

After this, Jake turned up to visit nearly every day, almost always with flowers or some special gift in his hands, always with an idea to spend the day fishing, hike up a mountain, picnic in a meadow, go horseback riding, read books in the cabin, or take a leisurely walk around the farm. Sometimes he only wanted to sit by her side reading, while she wrote words in her notebooks. Josie found him handy with repairing fences or handling most any tool, and she and her sisters quickly became accustomed to his visits. He jumped into the fray of whatever needed done around Cherry Crossing, often without being asked. Sometimes he invited Josie or all of them to dine at the mansion, attend a play at the theater, enjoy a carriage ride, or browse the town library to see if a new addition had escaped their notice. He brought the carriage around on Sunday mornings to drive them all to church, and Josie enjoyed sitting beside him on the pew. Sometimes she invited him to join them for a meal at the cabin after church, and other times, they dined as Jake's guests. A few times, they dined in town on Friday or Saturday evenings.

Jacqueline lamented the fact she had lost another beau, especially since Charlie Martin had cooled somewhat in his regard for her, but she kept herself busy making a new dress, and keeping up with the sewing she took in. Jillian threw herself into studying for her teaching certificate, hoping to take the required school board examination before Christmas.

In June, the election for mayor took place, despite the fact no other candidate had stepped up to run in opposition to Jake. Townsfolk turned out in record numbers to cast their votes for him, but they had an option to write in any other name, although no one did. They wrote Jake Hunter's name on a scrap of paper and tossed it inside the clear glass, empty pickle jar situated between Sheriff Drummond and "Deputy Padre," their pistols at the ready in case of any disputes. At the end of the day, Sheriff Drummond counted all the votes in the presence of Father Cornelius and declared Jake the winner.

Josie decided to take some time off from working at the mission to enjoy getting to know Jake and spend time on her writing and tend the farm, but Mother Marta said she could return whenever she liked. "You'll also be delighted to know Padre Cornelius has made an announcement."

"He has? What sort of an announcement?" Josie observed the children playing a game of Blind Man's Bluff outside.

"The children and any staff who wish may attend the summer dance in July, and the Wild West show," Marta said.

"What changed his mind?" Josie asked. "The children must be so happy."

"Oh, they are thrilled. The decision came after we received a sizeable donation for new clothing for the children specifically to purchase something to wear to the dance and enough left to pay for a ticket to the show for each adult and child at the mission." Mother Marta crossed her arms. "Would you care to know who made the donation?"

Josie nodded. "Of course, I am curious indeed."

"Jake Hunter made the donation. He also replenished our pantry and smokehouse with the items we used for the banquet, so we still have the resources we need to make it through winter. Of course, we need to work hard at our kitchen garden and canning items, but we are tremendously thankful. Except you mustn't let on knowing I've divulged this information. These kinds of things are, shall we say, private?" Marta smiled approvingly.

"Yes, of course, and I am pleased to hear it, and not surprised at the answer. He is more like his grandfather each day. I didn't know at first, but he is a true hero." Jocelyn smiled as she observed the children, happy to hear about Jake's deeds of kindness. The man followed in his grandfather's footsteps.

Upon reading the official result in the *Honey River Gazette* announcing he'd won the election, Jake saddled two horses and rode out to Cherry Crossing on the very next June morning to help with the cherry tree harvest. He found Josie on the wooden swing under the orchard. She stopped swinging when he reached her, surprised to see him holding the lead to Blue while he rode one of his grandfather's other horses. She looked so pretty sitting there on the swing, wearing a pink calico bonnet, her hair pinned up, ready to face the day.

"You're early, Jake," she said sweetly, a smile lighting up her face to see him. It hit him then, he hadn't thought of Clara in weeks. Yes, Jocelyn Hayes had consumed him, and he could hardly wait to show her what he'd brought. *Would she like it? Would she be pleased?*

"What brings you to Cherry Crossing in this manner, Mayor Hunter?" Josie teased as she reached to the ground for the copy of the newspaper she'd read earlier. She held it up for him to see the paper, and he smiled, dismounting. Her eyes, however, quickly took in the fact he'd brought Blue along, but she wondered why he hadn't ridden him.

"I guess it's official. I'm the new mayor of Honey River Canyon. I thought maybe you'd have started harvesting the cherries already. I thought I was late," he said.

She shook her head. "No, we are early. I only came to enjoy the swing and some time with the Lord before it gets busy today. A few friends are coming to help us as I mentioned previously, and Jillian will soon immerse herself in the kitchen making several batches of cherry jam, cherry preserves, and cherry cake, scones, pies, and muffins. I'll bounce between her progress and the orchard, checking to make sure we leave the stems on the cherries, and ensuring we don't forget to harvest one of the trees."

"We're supposed to leave the stems on?" he asked, pulling her to her feet. He clasped her hands in his and looked into her eyes.

She nodded. "Leaving the stems on helps the fruit last longer. Kind of like when we have accepted Jesus in our hearts. He's our stem, but if we aren't careful to keep Him close, we can be exposed to the harsh elements of life. It's the way Pa taught us, so I guess I always think of it this way." She paused. "He had all kinds of sermons about cherry trees. He used to say we are Kingdom transplants like these trees he brought from Canada. We are grafted into His Kingdom when we are born again. In turn, we have these amazing benefits, like His daily care and provision for us."

"It's what I love about you, Josie. Your faith. I woke up this morning, and I knew I could wait no longer to ask you to marry me." Jake surprised her then, kneeling on bended knee. He handed her the reins to Blue. "First of all, here is our horse. You may keep him here at Cherry Crossing. He belongs here with Mrs. Velvet."

Josie's mouth dropped open. "You're letting Blue come here early? Before we are even wed?"

He nodded. "Yes, you may have Blue at Cherry Crossing now."

She grinned, her eyes dancing. "You're calling him Blue!"

Jake nodded again. "I am. Tornado doesn't really fit the personality of this horse. He's been Blue since the first day you named him, and I was just too stubborn to admit it, but the name does suit him, the way his coat shines and all. It does have a kind of blue sheen to it."

Josie smiled, hardly believing she held the lead to Blue in her hands. Jake produced a lovely vintage ring from his pocket. "This ring belonged to my mother. She told me to give it to the woman I love one day, the one I want to spend the rest of my life with, the one I want to serve, love, provide for, and protect for all of my days. Jocelyn, will you marry me? I plan to make you the happiest girl in all of Montana."

"Oh, Jake! Of course, I'll marry you!" Josie threw her arms around him, tears of joy filling her eyes, one streaming down her rosy cheeks. "You already have made me the happiest girl in all of Montana."

The End

Author Note

Dear Reader,

I hope you enjoyed this story about Jocelyn Hayes. I'm looking forward to writing the next two books in this series about each of Josie's sisters and I look forward to sharing them with you. I particularly enjoyed writing about the nuns and priests at the mission in this fictional Christian romance novel.

It doesn't seem right to leave out a mention of my research about missions in the Western Hemisphere. This part of my research inspired the fictional St. Paul's Mission in Cherry Crossing. Florida boasted one of the oldest missions at St. Augustine. Puerto Rico, New Orleans, California, Oregon, and Montana also had missions, and certainly, others existed elsewhere.

Catholic churches from various dioceses in many of the colonial states and later in the Midwest, such as Toledo and Cincinnati, for instance, helped to found missions during the westward expansion. I read fascinating accounts about various buildings, bishops, nuns, their clothing, and volunteers who assisted them. It all served to spark my imagination. St. Paul's Mission came together in my mind when I wondered if some of these missions and Catholic churches communicated by letter and eventually worked together to found a western mission.

Building these characters prompted me to think of the various backgrounds each nun and priest might have. I cannot, however, imagine their level of devotion, how hard they must have worked, and the great sacrifice they made to spread the gospel of Jesus Christ.

Warmest Regards,

Lisa M. Prysock

Lisa's Recipe for Cherry Scones

The secret to this recipe is using cold butter, and don't work or mix the dough for too long once you add the wet ingredients.

Ingredients

2 cups flour

2 tablespoons sugar

3 teaspoons baking powder

½ teaspoon salt

1/3 cup cold, real butter, unsalted.

1 egg

¾ cup milk

½ cup dried cherries

Directions

Preheat oven to 425 degrees.

Mix flour, sugar, baking powder and salt. If your baking powder is more than six months old, add an extra teaspoon to make sure your scones rise and are light and fluffy.

Add the cold butter to the flour mixture. I like to cut the

stick of butter into slices before adding, making it easier to mix. Use a knife or a pastry cutter to mix together until the mixture has a coarse, grainy feel, like cornmeal.

In a separate bowl, beat the egg and milk together. Add this to the flour mixture and stir quickly until no flour shows. If the dough is not soft enough, add a little more milk. Quickly mix in the cherries. Remember not to overmix the dough. *If you substitute dried cherries with maraschino cherries, remember to rinse and pat them dry or your scones will be pink. They can affect the scone recipe slightly if you don't use dried cherries.

Place the dough on a floured surface and knead it gently about twelve to fifteen times.

Shape the dough into a ball, pressing down until evenly flat.

Use a circle-shaped cutter to cut out the scones. The number of scones will depend on the size of the cutter. I like to use a small two-inch diameter cutter. Another tip: don't twist the cutter when cutting the scones or they will bake lopsided.

Place these on a greased cookie sheet, not touching. Bake 10-12 minutes until golden brown. Serve warm with jam and butter or clotted cream, whipped cream, or your favorite toppings.

Try other variations to the recipe such as leaving the cherries out for plain scones, or you try adding other fruits and flavors to adapt the recipe. Best served warm.

Author Biography

Lisa M. Prysock is a *USA Today* Bestselling, Award-Winning Christian and Inspirational Author. She and her husband of more than twenty years reside in Kentucky. They have five children, grown.

She writes in the genres of both Historical Christian Romance and Contemporary Christian Romance, including a multi-author Western Christian Romance series, "Whispers in Wyoming." She is also the author of a devotional. Lisa enjoys sharing her faith in Jesus through her writing.

Lisa has many interests, but a few of these include gardening, cooking, drawing, sewing, crochet, cross stitch, reading, swimming, biking, and walking. She loves dollhouses, cats, horses, butterflies, hats, boots, flip-flops, espadrilles, chocolate, coffee, tea, chocolate, the colors peach and purple, and everything old-fashioned.

She adopted the slogan of "The Old-Fashioned Everything Girl" because of her love for classic, traditional, and old-fashioned everything. When she isn't writing, she can sometimes be found teaching herself piano and violin, but finds the process "a bit slow and painful." Lisa enjoys working with the children and youth in her local church creating human videos, plays, or programs incorporating her love for inspirational dance. A few of her favorite authors include Jane Austen, Lucy Maude Montgomery, Louisa May Alcott, and Laura Ingalls Wilder. You'll find "food, fashion, fun, and faith" in her novels. Sometimes she includes her own illustrations.

She continues the joy and adventure of her writing journey as a member of ACFW (American Christian Fiction Writers) and LCW (Louisville Christian Writers). Lisa's books are clean and wholesome, inspirational, romantic, and family oriented. She gives a generous portion of the proceeds to missions.

Discover more about this author at **www. LisaPrysock.com** where you'll find the links to purchase more of her books, free recipes, devotionals, author video interviews, book trailers, giveaways, blog posts, and much more, including an invitation to sign up for her free newsletter.

Links to Connect with Lisa:
https://www.facebook.com/LisaMPrysock
https://twitter.com/LPrysock
www.LisaPrysock.com
https://www.amazon.com/-/e/B00J6MBC64
(Lisa's page at Amazon Author Central.)

https://www.bookbub.com/authors/lisa-m-prysock
https://www.facebook.com/groups/500592113747995/
(Lisa's Facebook Reader & Friends group.)

Other Books by This Author

Author Tip--: View all of these books at www.LisaPrysock.com at the carousel on the home page of Lisa's website. Click on any book cover to view the product page at Amazon.

To Find a Duchess, an Inspirational Regency Romance

The Christian Victorian Heritage Series:

Hannah's Garden: a Turn of the Century Love Story

Abigail's Melody

The Lydia Collection

The Redemption of Lady Georgiana

Protecting Miss Jenna

Persecution & Providence

Arise Princess Warrior, a 30 Day Devotional Challenge

The Shoemaker, an Old-Fashioned Regency Christmas Story

Whispers in Wyoming, Contemporary Western Romance

Dreams of Sweetwater River

Marry Me Katie

No Place Like Home

All That Glitters

The Legend of Lollipop

Holly for Christmas

Lost in Wyoming

Secret Admirer

Becoming Princess Olivia, a Royal Contemporary Romance

Brides of Grace Hill, Generational Series Historical Saga

Geneva

Annabelle

Victoria

Tracy Jo, Coming Soon...

Brides of Pelican Rapids, Mail Order Bride Series

Lottie's True Love

Jenny's Secret Diary

Belle of the Ball

Josiah's Jewel

Silver Aspen

The Prairie Princess

Hazel's Tribulations

Holliday Island Resort

Blitzen the CEO

North and South

Minnesota Bride

Georgia Peaches

A Persevering Heart

A New Heart

An Anthology of Short Stories

Heartland Treasures

Billionaires & Debutantes

When We Dance

When It Storms

Westward Home & Hearts

Lydia's Lot

Charity's Challenge

Mistaken Identity Mail Order Brides

A Bride for Lane

An Impostor for Christmas

Mail Order Ramona

You Are on the Air

Dial F for Family: Sweet Christian Contemporary Romance Novella

Made in the USA
Middletown, DE
11 July 2022

69002072R00136